Breaking the Rules

Other Books by
EMMA LEIGH REED

EMMA LEIGH REED

Breaking the Rules

ELRpublishing

Text copyright © 2018 by Emma Leigh Reed
All rights reserved.

Published by ELR Publishing.

ISBN-13: 978-1-944550-09-7

Cover and interior design by Kenny Holcomb
kennyholcombdesigns.com

Printed in the United States of America

To my Jack

I could not have done this book without you. Your support and encouragement has pushed me to do the hard work. I can't thank you enough for the pep talks when I was convinced I couldn't do it, the continuous encouragement, and the ever-present sarcastic banter. No one can give it right back to me like you can! Thank you for showing me gracious forgiveness and friendship. This book has healed me in ways most people will never understand. I can't imagine my life without you.

one

I sat in the dark at the dining room table. A streak of moonlight cut through the curtains and illuminated the bottle of aspirin spilt out in front of me. Pill by pill washed down with a glass of wine; failure after failure swallowed until the bottle was almost gone.

Numbness overcame me and I laid my head on the table, watching the shadows deepen in the room. The voice of my roommate penetrated the silence, yet it sounded so far away. I closed my eyes and allowed myself to drift into the dark void . . .

Blinding lights sent a splintering pain through my head. My throat burned, and an aching throb wrenched my stomach. Finding myself in a hospital bed, I closed my eyes in resignation.

Failure again.

The story of my life. No matter what I tried, I couldn't seem to get anything right.

Tears rolled down my cheeks as I sighed. I'd only wanted one thing in life growing up, but love didn't exist for me, in any form whether it be from my parents or from an outsider. I was apparently bound here on this earth, withering a little more with every unbearable day, for even in my darkest hour I hadn't found a reprieve.

"Morning, Isabelle. How're you feeling?" The cheery nurse that invaded the room was too much to handle.

"Can you shut the shades, please?" I squinted as I watched her tidy the room and groaned quietly.

"Come on now. You need to get up and going this morning. How about a hot shower?" The nurse continued to putter around the room, pulling the shades farther open so the sunlight shown directly onto my bed.

"Maybe later. When am I being discharged?" I lifted my right arm and shielded my eyes.

"The doctor will be in shortly to talk to you. I would imagine your parents are on their way." The nurse stopped next to the bed and reach over to gently pull my arm away from my face. "Sweetie, we're all so glad you're okay."

I rolled my eyes and turned my head away. Great, just what I needed—pity. I laid silent, willing the nurse to leave the room. Once the door shut, I stood shakily and shuffled to the windows where I drew the shades closed.

Darkness. All I wanted was to retreat into it.

The voice in the back of my head started to nag. It didn't quit, even when I tried to drown it out. The needling reminder of what a failure I was, of how I would never be important to anyone in this life and would never find success. I'd heard the words so often they were second nature now and I believed them more than the hope of ever moving on and away to start over.

I heard my mother coming down the hallway long

before she entered the room. She strode toward my bed, put together as usual, her lips pinched in that perpetual disappointed look. My father followed and shut the door behind him.

Here it comes.

I steeled myself.

And waited.

"What do you have to say for yourself?" Her ice-cold voice broke the silence in the room.

I didn't answer, just closed my eyes.

"Isabelle, what happened?" Dad's voice was tender and quiet, the polar opposite to my mother. How on earth those two ever came to be together, I couldn't imagine.

"I apparently took too many aspirin last night." I shrugged and sat up, then looked him in the eyes, pleading silently to let the matter drop. "Can we leave now?"

"How could you do this to us?" My mother's strained voice spoke volumes of the burden I was to the family.

"I'm sorry. Of course, I wasn't thinking." My heart broke. It was just one more reminder that it had nothing to do with me or my feelings, it was always about my mother and how things impacted her.

"Don't be—" My mother's words were cut off as the doctor came into the room. He looked between my parents, then back to me. Pointedly ignoring them, he crossed the room and stopped at the edge of the bed.

"Isabelle, how are you this morning? Do we need a moment alone?" His eyes locked onto mine and I couldn't pull away. Did he sense the tension in the room?

I shook my head *no*.

"Doctor, we're her parents. What can we do and when can we take her home?" I shot a glance toward my mother, startled by the sudden sympathetic tone of her voice.

"I need to speak with Isabelle for a few minutes, so if you'll just step outside. Then I'll talk to all of you together." The doctor motioned toward the door and ignored the killing look my mother threw at him.

"I'm sure Isabelle would want us to stay while you talk to her." Mother glanced at my father as if willing him to step in, yet he just stood there looking at me. The doctor was not to be persuaded, or bullied, and insisted they leave.

With the room finally quiet, Dr. Erikson sat on the edge of the bed. "Let's talk, Isabelle."

"I've got nothing to say."

He nodded. "You know, I'm not sure it's healthy for you to keep this all in. Obviously, something is bothering you and I might have a guess as to what it could be, but it certainly would help if you would tell me."

"Nothing is bothering me. Can I go home?" I folded my arms across my chest, defiance oozing even in the pathetic hospital gown.

The doctor made notes on my chart and handed me a piece of paper. "My office number if you want to talk. I'm going to recommend you see someone who can help you sort this out."

I shook my head. "There's nothing to sort out. Please, save both of our times and don't bother referring me anywhere. I won't go."

"I'll discharge you. You can get dressed and I'll go over the details with your parents, if I have your permission. I don't have to tell them anything. You are eighteen."

"Whatever. I don't care." Snarkiness crept into my voice. "Go ahead and tell her, it will save me from being badgered on the drive home." I closed my eyes again, trying to hold back the tears that threatened to spill over my lashes.

I took a deep breath.

Feeling in control again, I glanced down at the discharge papers and read the words YOU'RE NOT ALONE sprawled across the bottom. How naïve was this doctor? He didn't have a clue about my life and how alone I really was. I'd been alone in this family since I was twelve years old.

The drive home was uneventful. Silence filled the car and tension was thick. I laid back in my seat with eyes closed, praying that my parents would think I was asleep and leave me alone.

We'd no sooner walked into the house when the tirade began. Although the words were directed at my father, I knew they were for me. I continued through the house to my bedroom, but Mother's voice just got louder and louder.

"How could she do this to us? What are people going to think? That we're bad parents and we didn't know how to raise her? After all we've done for her, she pulls this stunt? She doesn't have the right to be happy after this. God help us, I will make sure she is *never* happy."

Sitting on the edge of my bed, I listened to mother drone on and on. My poor father. Every so often I'd hear him say "Now, now, it'll be okay," then Mother would just start in again; over and over the same lecture. Each time those words came to my ears, my heart broke a little more. Why couldn't they see it had nothing to do with them? I wanted to scream *THIS IS ABOUT ME*, but I knew it would fall on deaf ears. Those same ears that had been closed to anything I'd tried say for the past six years.

Every fear shoved aside, every insecurity brought to light and exploited.

I sighed. I needed more than anything to simply disappear.

I wouldn't be allowed to go back to college now. I was stuck in this house where I didn't belong . . . never had.

A gripping pain doubled me over. I curled into the fetal position and pulled a blanket over me, then drifted off to sleep dreaming of being in a family where I was loved and cared for, wondering how I could miss what I'd never known.

two

Weeks had passed since I went to my parents' home from the hospital. I spent day after day walking miles through the woods and trails that wound around the running brook behind our house. When I wasn't walking, I was locked in my room, sitting on the floor listening to music. I repeatedly played songs of lost love or misguided love and wondered how people knew when they were *in* love.

My parents never mentioned the suicide attempt again. I'd hear Mother tell people that I had given up on college, not knowing what I wanted to do, and had decided to come home until I knew what avenue I was going to pursue. It all sounded good and people bought into the fact that poor Isabelle just didn't know what she wanted in life. It certainly had nothing to do with my childhood and how unhappy I was. But then again, I'd perfected the façade of letting everyone see a well-balanced young woman who was always happy and cheerful.

It made me sick to know that I was good at playing the part, when inside all I wanted was someone to hold me and tell me I was going to be okay. Life didn't have to be perfect, just a little better than it was at this moment. And honestly, I couldn't have been any lower in my life. My heart hurt constantly from the ache of being alone. I was exhausted from the depression that had taken over my body and mind. The only time I felt any sense of peace was when I was hiking through the trails, away from the sound of my mother's voice.

But here in New England you can only get outside so much, as fall turns into winter. The leaves turned in color to the vibrant golds and reds. I loved autumn, when the leaves were on the ground. The crunching beneath my feet gave me a sense of trampling the bad beneath me and moving on. But like all good things, they come to an end. When deer season started, I could no longer take those daily walks in the woods.

I spent more and more time in my room, locked away from everyone. I could hear my parents talking and Mother repeatedly complaining that "Isabelle's is simply *trying* to hurt us by withdrawing." As much as I couldn't stand to hear the negative comments, I couldn't bring myself to spend time with them.

The one thing I couldn't escape was the demand that I attend church every Sunday. Maybe my parents thought my soul could still be saved, although I had been told suicide was the ultimate unforgivable sin. So, I sat every Sunday, week after week, the sinner on the back pew. Thankfully my parents had relented and allowed me to park myself alone in church instead of with them.

December arrived and the first snow. I sat in the back pew, freezing. The old church didn't hold heat and every time the door opened behind me, the cold air blew right down my neck. It was still warmer than sitting next to my mother. I pulled my sweater closer around me and hunched over, pretending to look through the hymnal.

I glanced up as a young family walked in. The mother and children had been coming regularly. But the young man with them was new. I watched with fascination. The jeans fit him well and he wore a plaid button-down shirt over a solid turtleneck, carrying his bomber jacket over his arm. He smiled at one of the kids and his dimples deepened and drew my attention. I'd never seen anyone in this small town like him before and certainly not in this church.

I looked back to the hymnal as the young mother talked to my parents, then slipped into the pew behind them. I stole glances at the young man. My face flushed as I became aware of him watching me. I wanted to run, but there was something about him that drew me in. I couldn't keep my eyes off him, and when he flashed those dimples at me, an odd warmth spread through my heart.

The service dragged on like every other Sunday and as the congregation finally sang the closing hymn, I was already looking for a way to escape before having to speak to anyone. It had become one of many irritations to my mother—the only prompt needed. I had gotten to the point over the last few weeks that whatever I could do to tick my mother off, I did. I thrived on tormenting her with the agony of having a rebel child that brought about talk of the town. But this morning, I was inclined to take my time. I slowly slipped my jacket on, looping the buttons one at a time in a leisurely fashion when the young man reached the opening of the pew.

"Hey. I'm Jack." He flashed those dimples and I knew I would never be the same.

"Isabelle."

He nodded. "My sister told me."

I met his eyes and was taken back by the blueness of them. Dimples and blue eyes, I was a goner for sure. "Did you just move here?"

"I'm stationed at the Air Force base on the coast. Just spending my off weekend at my sister's." He leaned against the back of the pew in front of them, making no effort to leave.

I sat down, not breaking eye-contact. Words I wanted to say stuck in my throat and instead of speaking, I stared like a dumb girl who couldn't put a sentence together. He finally stood tall and stepped out of the pew. I pulled myself up and took a step forward, but stopped suddenly when he turned back toward me.

"It was nice to meet you, Isabelle." He grinned again and I smiled.

"You, too."

I slipped out of the pew and headed for the door. I could hear my mother apologizing for her rude daughter. I paused briefly. The grin spread over my face when I heard Jack inform my mother that I had been anything, but rude. It was a rare man who wasn't afraid to contradict what my mother said.

I slipped into my parents' car, waiting patiently while they talked to different people. I watched as Jack left, talking with his niece and nephew. At least I hadn't been invisible to him, but I also didn't imagine he would be back. He was here just for the weekend and there was no point fantasizing about the impossible. Ha, look at me sounding just like my mother.

Finally home, I escaped to my room once again. It had been almost a month since *the night*. The migraine was back. I drew the blinds and laid on the bed, willing it to subside. Beside the bed was a glass of water and two Advil. I was no longer allowed to have a bottle of pain relief anywhere near me. Mother insisted I come to her and ask for any pills if needed. The pills had been sitting there since yesterday. I could stock pile them to use, but I knew that I would never go that route again. I couldn't even take those two for the headache that split my head wide open. Every time I attempted to take something, my throat closed. I would rather suffer from the pain than attempt to swallow another pill. It was as if my body was protecting me from myself and the depression that overtook daily.

I must have drifted off to sleep. I awoke with a start to mother banging on the door. "Isabelle, telephone."

I sat up cautiously. The migraine had subsided, but I knew if I got up too quickly it would hit hard again.

"Isabelle, did you hear me?" Her impatience evident.

"Yup. I'm coming." I opened the door to have Mother blocking my path. "Who is it?"

"That young man from church this morning. Don't be rude." Mother handed me the cordless phone and I waited until she moved down the hall before I shut the door.

"Hello?"

"It's Jack . . . from this morning." The deep voice came through the phone and reached down to the core of me.

"Hi, Jack. What's up?"

"I'm here until tomorrow. Thought maybe you'd like to go grab a pizza tonight or something."

I clenched the phone to my ear. He was asking me out! My heart raced as I tried to focus on what to say. "Um, sure. Okay."

His quiet chuckle came across the line. "Do I make you nervous?"

I smiled at the question. I *was* nervous and couldn't figure out why. "No, of course not." I put him at ease with my usual I'm-good-cheerful-self and internally cringed.

"Good. I'll pick you up at five."

"Okay. See you then." I softly clicked the off button to the phone after giving him quick directions to the house, then leaned against the door and sighed.

I opened the door to take the phone back to its base. Both parents looked up from the books they were reading as I entered the living room.

"What did he want?" Mother asked. I couldn't tell if she was disgusted that he had actually called or if just maybe she was pleased.

"We're going to go get some pizza."

"We don't even know him, Isabelle." Dad spoke up.

"You know his sister. He's only here until tomorrow and he doesn't know anyone his age. God, it's not a marriage proposal, it's just pizza." I turned and fled back to my room. It was always the same argument, never giving me any support to go out and be social.

I plugged in my curling iron. I was going to have fun tonight, regardless of what my parents thought. I just needed to get leave, away from them, to give myself a chance to have some excitement without the oppression that was over me all the time. It was a dark cloud that only lifted when I was out with friends.

I spent the next hour curling my hair and putting on make-up. I chose a new pair of jeans and a jade-green sweater to wear. The green brought out the green in my eyes. I loved this color as it made me feel attractive. The way my eyes changed color with what I wore had always seemed weird, but when I wore green and my eyes turned to this particular shade, I felt empowered and good about myself. Simple things . . . it was always the simple things that brought me a small amount of joy.

The doorbell rang right at five o'clock. He was punctual at least and my parents wouldn't be able to find fault with that. I heard Dad asking where we were going and Jack gave the appropriate answers. Although I was eighteen, my parents made it clear I had an early curfew because it was a work day tomorrow. For the love of God, why did they feel the need to do that to me?

I entered the living room and stopped short. Jack was dressed in jeans, that fit him perfectly, and a blue sweater. The blue made his eyes shine like pools of water and I felt myself slipping. I smiled and tried to will away the heat from my face.

"Hi, Jack." I walked to his side. "Ready?"

"Isabelle, nine o'clock. Not a minute later." Dad spoke to me, but his eyes never left Jack.

"Dad . . . that's ridiculous."

"My house, my rules."

I shrugged and turned apologetically to Jack. He flashed those dimples. "No worries."

He was ever the gentleman, opening the car door for me and waiting until I settled before shutting it and going around to the driver's side. We rode in silence until we left the limits of the small town, headed to the closest pizza joint two towns over.

"I'm sorry." I started.

"Don't. Don't apologize for your parents. I don't care that they're protective." Jack reached for my hand and squeezed it. Although his grip loosened, he left his hand covering mine. The warmth from him spread through me and I relaxed. I turned my hand over so my palm faced his. Our fingers intertwined. Not a word needed to be spoken. It was as if his heart spoke to mine. I drew in a deep breath and exhaled. The immediate connection between us crackled in the air around us.

"You okay now?" His voice was quiet, laced with concern.

"Of course. My parents need to let go and I just hate it when it spills over onto other people." The statement touched only the minute tip of what the real issue was, but I couldn't let him know the depth of the control my parents sought to keep over me.

"It's no big deal. They see a young military man and they're concerned for their daughter." I knew Jack meant well, but he just didn't know what their motivation truly was. I held his hand tighter and rubbed my thumb over his in small circular motions.

"Let's not talk about them. Tell me about you." I turned to look at him. His dimple deepened as he smiled, and drew me in. I gazed at him, taking in every feature. The short military haircut, the smile, the blue eyes.

"Not much to tell. Been in the Air Force a couple of years now. Just got stationed here in New Hampshire, which I'm glad because now I'm close to my sister and can see the kids more often."

I looked around. The place was quiet with it being Sunday, which I was grateful for. There would be no one here that could report back to my parents. I smiled at him and wondered how to start the conversation.

Fortunately, the pizza arrived quickly, allowing me to get my wits about me.

"What are you studying in college?" Jack broke the silence.

"I was studying business, but I'm taking some time off."

Jack studied me for a moment. "Why?"

I smiled. "Not sure exactly what I want to do, so it doesn't make sense to spend the money for college." My mother would have been proud the way I kept in line with her lies.

He nodded as he took another bite. I took a bite while he chewed and then asked, "What are you going to do?"

"Find a job, I guess." I shrugged. "God knows I can't stand to be in that house for any length of time."

"Want to talk about that?"

"My home life…no, thanks." I laughed. "Trust me, that's a short conversation and not very interesting."

Jack flashed those dimples. Life suddenly was better just looking at that smile. "Come on, it can't be that bad."

I pondered that and locked eyes with him. How to respond to that? He wouldn't understand the dysfunctionality of my family of origin. "I guess it depends on your perspective."

"That's very true. And I really shouldn't say anything. I don't know you well enough to know what goes on there. I'm hoping to get to know you better though."

"Let's start with you. What made you want to be in the service?" Safe conversation, not about me, was always a good thing.

"Reasons I don't want to bore you with," he joked. "I needed something to ensure I could find success in my life. Home life wasn't the best and the military seemed like a good option."

"Home life…I guess everyone has their own demons

they battle on that front." I mused. "How are you liking it so far?"

"The Air Force? I love it. I'm feeling like I'm doing something with my life that has purpose."

"I wonder sometimes what purpose my life has." I spoke the words out loud and immediately wished I could take them back.

"It will come to you, I'm sure. Don't be so hard on yourself." He spoke softly. I wanted to believe those words more than anything, but somehow my past wasn't allowing me to take anything on faith these days.

Jack held my hand again on the ride home and I resisted the urge to slide to the middle of the bench seat to be close to him. I wanted to feel his warmth, feel like something was going right in my life for a change. I contented myself with the feel of his hand in mine, the warmth it gave me and the gentleness.

He came around and opened my car door when we arrived home and walked me to the house. Inside the garage, I stopped just shy of the steps. It was out of the window's view and I didn't want to take the chance of my parents watching us.

"I really had fun tonight, Jack."

He stepped closed to me. "I did, too. Can I see you again?"

I looked up to meet his eyes. "How is that going to work when you live an hour away?"

He smiled. "I have three weekends a month off and I'll be spending those weekends at my sister's house. I want to see you." His hands reached for my hips and pulled me a step closer to him.

I smiled as I slid my hands up his biceps. "I'd like that."

He leaned forward and gently brushed his lips against mine. The kiss was brief and tender, and he pulled his head back just a moment to gaze into my eyes, before he came back in and captured my lips with his. I sighed softly as I pulled him closer, sliding my hand around his neck. His tongue teased my lips and I opened my mouth to allow him entrance. He was demanding, and yet gentle and teasing. We pulled apart and I reluctantly slid my arms back down his biceps as I relinquished my hold on him.

"I'll call you tomorrow when I get back to the barracks." He turned toward his car and I stood there watching him walk away, my lips tingling.

I smiled, then headed for the door as his car backed out of the driveway.

This was a night I would never forget.

three

The next couple of weeks were a whirlwind. I started a new job as a secretary for a law firm and enjoyed learning the new aspects of my job. I thrived at the office, away from the heavy scrutiny of my parents, and received praise from all I worked with at how fast I picked up things, and how detail oriented I was.

The nights were spent locked up in my bedroom, listening to music, thinking of Jack. He'd called me every other night. Our conversations were short, but I loved hearing his voice and knowing he was thinking of me. He had worked the past weekend and now coming up on Friday, he would be in town. I tingled with anticipation of seeing him again.

We hadn't seen each other since that kiss that had left me feeling giddy and unsteady for several days. My parents had quizzed me about what was going on, but

I was vague and made it sound like I was only talking to him because he knew no one else in the area. That seemed to pacify them for the moment, but they had expressed their displeasure at the fact that I had a date with him this weekend.

I moved through the days with ease at work and grimaced at my time at home. I looked into apartments and battled with my parents about moving out. I was constantly told I couldn't afford it, or that it wasn't in my best interest to live by myself. I knew that was a direct hit regarding the suicide attempt, although it was never discussed. I'd found out that the doctor had told my parents not to bring it up, knowing full well they were not supportive. But on some level that hurt, too. It was like it was brushed aside as something unimportant.

And yet it defined me. It was the pinnacle of who I had become and how my life had shaped me. I couldn't get past the fact that I still felt like my own life was a personal failure and I never would find happiness. Although I had glimpses of what it would be like to be happy – every time I heard Jack's voice.

Friday dragged. I checked the clock every five minutes, knowing full well Jack wouldn't be in town until close to six. I would be home from work around five-thirty. He was going to pick me up on his way in, and we were going to have dinner at his sister's house. It was a safe thing to do, one my parents didn't question as they liked his sister.

I was changed and ready. For once, I left the bedroom and waited in the living room for Jack to arrive. My parents made small talk and we talked at ease about my job. As the subject came around to Jack, my mother took that pinched look to her face and her tone was harsh.

"Don't be doing anything that gives him the impression you're easy."

I felt like I'd been slapped. "What do you mean?"

"You know what I mean. Kissing him, leading him on. Those service guys think they can have sex whenever they want it."

"And how would you know that?" The words slipped out before I thought about it.

"Are you getting smart with me?" Mother stood.

I took a deep breath. "I'm just saying you don't know Jack. He's looking for a friend. And obviously, you don't know me, either." I stood as I saw the headlights of Jack's car swing into the driveway.

"Curfew is still in place, Isabelle." Dad's voice broke the silence.

"I think with it being Friday night, Dad, that nine is a little early. Don't worry. I won't be late and you know where I am." I turned before he could reply and was out of the house before Jack even exited his car. He jumped out and ran around to open the door for me.

"Let's go." My teeth were clenched. There would be consequences later for being rude to my father. And if I showed up later than nine, there would definitely be hell to pay. But at this point, I didn't care. I just wanted to be with the man that made me feel at ease. He made me laugh and smile, something I hadn't done a lot of in years, unless I was in *show mode*.

"Bad day at work or at home?" Jack reached for my hand once we were on the road.

"I love my job." I responded.

"That's what I thought. Let's forget your parents for tonight. Just you and me . . ." He chuckled. ". . . at my sisters. The kids won't leave us alone. You realize that, right?"

I almost believed it. Jack and me, together against the world. It was a fantasy I allowed myself to think about a lot and yet I knew it would never happen.

The night progressed as planned. Laughter, family night of games with Jack and his sister, husband and kids. I almost felt like I was in a real family for a change. There were never these moments of pure silliness in my household. As the clock struck ten, my demeanor changed. It was time to get ready to go home. I was already past my curfew and although I'd pretty much told my parents I was going to be out later, I didn't dare push the limit too far.

I looked up to see Jack watching me. I tried to smile, but I dreaded leaving and having to face my parents.

"We should go." Jack pulled me to my feet. "Thanks, sis, for the fun."

I nodded. "Thank you."

Once in the car, Jack turned to me before starting it. "You okay?"

I nodded. "My parents are going to be pissed because I didn't come back at their curfew time."

"You told them you would be late, though."

I couldn't meet his eyes. "I know, but I don't think they believed I would actual defy them."

Jack's fingers ran along my jaw until under my chin, then he lifted my face until I made eye contact with his. "Why didn't you tell me? I don't want to get you in trouble."

My eyes filled with tears. "Please don't be mad at me . . . I don't want the night to end. I'm having fun."

Jack leaned forward and kissed me gently. "I'm not mad. I'm worried about you if your parents are upset."

I reached my hand behind his neck and pulled him closer. Our lips claimed each other and the heat level in the car ratcheted up a notch while I scooted closer to

Jack. As we broke from the kiss, Jack pulled me right up against him in the middle of the seat and simply folded me into his arms, holding me close.

I melted against him, drawing from him warmth and strength. "It'll be fine. They won't stay mad long. And it certainly won't be the first time they've been angry with me."

Jack pulled away to start the car, keeping one arm on my leg and holding me close to his side. We drove in silence back to the house. As we pulled into the driveway, Jack shut off the car and started to get out.

"Please, don't get out. You should go." I slid out of the passenger door and shut the door before Jack could say anything. I turned when I got to the stairs at the garage and gestured for him to leave before blowing him a kiss.

"You're late." I jumped as Dad spoke when I passed the living room.

"It's ten-thirty on a Friday night. That's hardly late for an eighteen-year-old." I stood still in the hallway, waiting for the fallout.

"I told you nine."

"And I told you I wasn't going to be late, but I wasn't going to be here at nine either. You knew where we were. Call the Millers and see what time we left." Frustration laced my voice and I wanted to scream at the top of my lungs at the injustice of it all.

"We'll talk about it in the morning." Dad dismissed me.

I shut my bedroom door and flopped down on the bed. I didn't want to be here anymore. It wasn't the thoughts of death that consumed me anymore. No, I had hope when I was with Jack, but still the negative influence in my life, in this house, was slowly killing me.

The next day the phone rang. I waited and waited for someone to come to my bedroom door and tell me

Jack was on the phone. Nothing. An hour or so later the phone rang again. I pulled open the bedroom door and started down the hall to hear mother on the phone saying "She's not here and won't be the rest of the day. You really don't need to call back, Jack."

I ran into the living room just as mother was hanging up the phone. "How could you?"

"You don't need this right now. You haven't even gotten your life together from . . . your college experience," My mother snapped.

"My college experience?" I snorted. "You mean my trying to kill myself?"

"Isabelle, that's enough."

"Is it? Who decides, Mother? You? It's not enough. You walk around like it never happened or like I fatally wounded you by doing such a thing. Guess what? It's not about you. Never was. This is *my* life and you need to stop interfering with it." My voice rose an octave as my raw nerves were finally exposed and there was no stopping the flow of the hurt and anger that was coming forth.

I didn't see my mother's hand until the palm struck me full force on the cheek. "Stop it."

I rubbed my stinging cheek. "You have no right to not let me talk to Jack. No right."

"I have every right. You live in my house, under my roof, and therefore you abide by my rules. He kept you out late last night." Mother spoke as if speaking to a five-year-old.

"He didn't do anything. We left when I told him I had to leave." I turned to walk away. "I don't have to live here if it's such an inconvenience for you," I muttered under my breath as I once again locked myself in the bedroom.

I never left my room other than to use the bathroom the rest of the day and night. Sunday morning I was woken by Mother knocking on the door telling me they were leaving in an hour for church and I was to be ready. I groaned, but inwardly I prayed that Jack would be at church.

I was dressed and waiting by the door when the hour was up. I said nothing to my parents as we got in the car and drove the short distance to church.

Mother turned in the car to me. "You will sit with us today."

I looked her directly in the eyes. "No, Mother. I will sit where I always do, by myself. You wouldn't want to tip off everyone that anything is different or wrong. It might cause questions that you don't want to answer." I slipped out of the car before she answered and walked to the front door of the church. I glanced behind me and saw my parents whispering beside the car before Dad took Mother's hand and they walked to the church with smiles on their faces.

Hypocrites.

I cringed and wandered inside.

I sat down in my usual pew in the back row. My parents walked by me to their usual spot and I breathed a sigh of relief. My nerves were raw and I tapped my fingers on my leg waiting, hoping, for Jack to show up. There was a flurry of activity at the door and I didn't bother to turn around. I needed to not watch for him. I closed my eyes briefly trying to shut off the emotions spinning within me.

I opened them as I felt a body sit down close to me. I glanced up and there was Jack, smile on his face. His hand reached for mine, entwining our fingers, giving them a little squeeze. He mouthed the words, "You okay?"

I nodded. "Now I am." I caught Mother glancing

back at me and I just smiled at her as I slid a fraction of an inch closer to Jack. Mother shot daggers at us and I wanted to laugh. Jack was a shield to her from the negativity, even if he didn't realize it. I wished I could open up to him and let him know my true self, not the happy-go-lucky persona I had adopted since that fateful night, maybe even earlier.

As they stood to sing the first song, Jack let go of my hand to put his arm around my waist and pulled me close so we could share the hymnal. I looked up to him and saw his dimples as he smiled down at me. The service for the first time in a long time seemed to go by too quickly and I had to find some way to spend more time with Jack.

"I'm sorry about yesterday," I whispered. "I was home."

Jack reached for my hand again. "No worries. I knew you were and figured this was their way of punishing you for rebelling against them. I hope they blamed me and not you."

I frowned. "They did, but I don't want them blaming you. It's me they have the issue with…not you."

"Isabelle, we're leaving." My mother and father were standing next to the pew.

"Jack and I are going to go grab something to eat. He'll bring me home." I knew it was a bold move since Jack hadn't mentioned doing something, but also too many people had heard me, and my parents couldn't argue about it.

They nodded and shot me a look. I knew I would pay for this and my saving grace was work tomorrow so I wouldn't be home.

"Thank you," Jack directed at my parents as we walked by and they simply gave a small head movement to indicate they heard him, but no other response.

"Sorry to put you on the spot," I murmured.

"Are you kidding? I was trying to figure out how to steal you away for the afternoon. How long do we have?"

"A few hours anyway. Probably should be home before dinner. What time do you need to head back to the base?"

"By six. If I have you home by four-thirty, it will give me plenty of time." Jack grinned at me. "I would love to take you to the coast and show you around the base some day when we have the full day."

"I'd love that." I felt a twinge of something unknown...happiness? Contentment? Whatever it was, I loved the feeling and wanted to hang on to it at all costs.

We drove to the mall and spent the next few hours simply strolling by the shops holding hands.

"What about after the service?" I asked.

"What do you mean?"

"What do you want to do? Where do you want to live?" I wanted to know everything that made this man tick.

"Air traffic control. It's the reason I'm in the service, to learn what I need to in order to work in the private sector. There's a need for them so I'll be able to find and keep work."

"Any airports special that you want to work at?" I was fascinated by the fact that he knew exactly what he wanted.

"Some place big -- Chicago maybe."

I listened mostly to Jack's dreams and only offered a few things about traveling. I really didn't know what I wanted in the future. It had been something I never thought about...a distant place that I really never thought I would get to.

"Don't you think of the future?" Jack interrupted my thoughts.

"Not really." I shrugged. "I just don't know…" I stopped and sat down on a bench. I watched Jack as he sat next to me.

"Why not?"

"Well, you've seen my home life. Doesn't give one much inspiration to think to the future."

Jack reached for my hand. "You're not the only one with a dysfunctional family. Have you ever heard anything about my family?"

I shook my head. "How would I have heard?"

"Didn't know if my sister had ever said anything." Jack sat back, holding my hand tight. "I know you have issues with your mother, but you're lucky to have one."

"That's debatable, but why would you say that?" I watched him closely.

Jack stared straight ahead, quiet. I sat silently waiting for him to speak. "I don't have much of a memory of my mother. She left when I was young."

"So it was just you, your dad and your sister?" I thought that couldn't have been so bad. I would do anything not to have to deal with my mother.

"Well, technically, yes. My sister really raised me. My dad blamed me for my mother's leaving so he was hands off. Really only spoke to me when he was angry." Jack sighed. He turned towards me. "No matter how bad your mother is, you have one."

"Honestly, I hate to say it, but you can have her. I know that may sound terrible to you, but she doesn't care about me one at all." I bit back my anger and tried to keep the tone light.

"How can you say she doesn't care? She's harsh, yes, but I'm sure she cares about you."

"You know when I was in middle school, I overheard her tell my father how she hated that she was stuck home raising me. She wanted her career and didn't want me." I shrugged. "I guess I just never feel like I fit in and maybe I don't. Obviously, she didn't want me. I must have been a mistake from the beginning."

Jack let go of my hand and put his arm around me, pulling me close. "You're not a mistake, Izzy."

Hearing my nickname, my breath caught in my throat. Only the closest people called me that. "Anyway…I envy you. You have your life plan all mapped out and at the age of twenty. Until I met you, I couldn't see my future at all."

We stood and started walking back to the car. Conversation turned to the upcoming Christmas holiday. He would be at his sister's but wanted to spend Christmas Eve with me. I invited him to church and dinner at our house afterwards.

The invite was already issued now so my parents wouldn't be able to renege on it without coming across as rude and since appearances were everything, I was going to push the boundaries. One of two things would happen, they would finally lighten up and accept who I was, or they wouldn't and I would move out and be on my own.

Being with Jack was easy. Nothing had ever come easy to me and this thing we had just flowed smoothly. I never felt such a connection with someone that I had only known for such a short time. In reality, we had only known each other about four weeks.

We planned for me to come with Jack to the base the Saturday after Christmas, so he could show me around. He was so proud of his military accomplishments and wanted to share them with me. My heart swelled like never before for the pleasure I gave him by showing interest or for the feelings of pride I had for him as he talked about what he was doing.

Plans were made final for Christmas Eve and the Saturday following for the two of us to be together. I sat close on the ride home and allowed myself to relax with my head on his shoulder.

four

Work had just a skeleton crew on the few days before Christmas, and I volunteered to be one that manned the office. I couldn't stand being home with just my parents and began putting in long hours for any excuse not to go home. Finally, Christmas Eve arrived and I stayed at my job only till noon. As I drove home, anticipation filled me at the thought of seeing Jack tonight.

My parents and I had come to a truce when it came to Jack. We agreed that I would have a bit more freedom within reason, as long as I didn't abuse it. I had agreed to it because that meant I would be able to see him any weekend he was off from work. I craved the sound of his voice during the week and it just wasn't always feasible for us to talk on the phone. The use of the payphone in the barracks got expensive.

Wearing a dress and boots, I looked in the mirror and smiled. I looked good and hoped that Jack would like the outfit. I spent a bit more of my paycheck than I should have on the outfit, but I wanted to impress him.

Jack stood outside of the church when we arrived, in a stance that took my breath away. I held a hand to my heart and took in the view. He looked so handsome in his dress blue uniform--something I had never seen him in before. Not only did he steal my breath away, when he finally spotted me and flashed those dimples, my knees weakened and my heart raced.

We walked into church, my hand tucked into the crook of his elbow. I never felt so proud of him as I did seeing him in that uniform. He stood tall and straight, and only a hint of dimples remained as he talked to people. It was like an air of seriousness that came with the uniform, until he looked at me. As if those dimples were saved just for me and every time he flashed them, my heart melted just a little bit more.

We sat in silence during the church service, palm to palm, fingers laced together. There was no room to get any closer in that aspect. My mind wandered throughout the service, wondering how I would make it through the next three days. I wanted to spend every minute with this man, not sporadically see him.

Once church was over, we walked to his car to head for my house. My parents were meeting us there along with my grandparents on my father's side for Christmas Eve dinner. There was an air of freedom around the house. Laughter between my parents and grandparents allowed Jack and I to pair off to the side and just enjoy each other. There were no remarks to call us into the other conversation.

As Jack sat in the overstuffed chair next to the fireplace, I sat down on his lap. He held me close, whispering about what we hoped to receive on Christmas. We had agreed not to buy each other presents since this relationship, if you could call it that, was so new between us. Four short weeks we had been seeing each other and I felt like it had been a lifetime since I met him.

After a little while, Jack and I started to the kitchen to clean up for my mother. Jack jumped right into washing the dishes after throwing a dish towel at me telling me to wipe, once again flashing his dimples. We talked quietly as we did the domestic thing of washing and drying, and then putting away the dishes. How could something feel so natural?

After my grandparents left, and my parents were sitting in the living room, Jack and I once again sat together in the overstuffed chair in the corner, enjoying the fire. I caught the odd looks my mother was giving me, and I couldn't read what they meant. I leaned my head on Jack's shoulder and allowed myself to be mesmerized by the flame. Jack's hands were clasped together around my waist, holding me tight.

As the clocked struck ten, Dad cleared his throat. Jack kissed me on the forehead. "I should go."

I looked up at him, willing him to stay, but knowing my parents were ready for him to leave. I simply nodded and stood.

"Thank you, sir, ma'am, for allowing me to spend the evening with Isabelle and your family. I had a great time."

Dad shook Jack's hand. "Anytime." I questioned if it was a sincere comment or not. Had they finally accepted Jack in my life or where they simply putting on a continued show? Even I couldn't always tell the fake from the real with my parents.

I walked Jack to the door and knew my parents were

watching us. Jack leaned forward and kissed me gently on the lips. "Merry Christmas, Isabelle."

"Merry Christmas, Jack." I grinned up at him. "I'll see you Saturday."

"I can't wait." Jack glanced quickly to the living room and my parents watching us. I could see he thought better of giving me another kiss and simply headed out the door giving my hand a quick squeeze as he left. I shut the door behind him, sighing softly.

"Really, Isabelle, you need to be more careful." Mother's voice cut through my moment of contentment.

"About what?"

"Sitting in his lap. You are pretty much telling him you are easy."

I sighed. "No, Mother, I'm not. He doesn't think that."

"You don't know what that boy thinks. He's twenty and you are a naïve little girl who thinks love is something that is all roses." Mother's voice grated on my nerves.

"Trust me, you have pretty much taught me love is quite the opposite." I fled up the hall to my room.

"Isabelle, you come back here!"

I shut the door and flipped the lock. I hurled myself on to the bed and allowed the tears to flow. In one small moment, the happiness of the evening was torn from me by my mother's cruel words. If she had her way, I would never be happy.

"Isabelle, open up." Dad's voice came through the door.

"I'm going to bed, Dad. I'm tired and we always get up early on Christmas." I turned over and faced the wall, tears rolling down my cheeks.

"Night then." Dad never was one to push me, yet he never stood up for me either. I had always felt close to my dad, yet always wondered why there hadn't been more.

Had he acted out of fear? Fear of his wife? Fear of conflict? I was just about ready to give up on my fears. I wanted to be fearless and yet I didn't know if I had the courage for it. There was only one way to find out. I was going to pursue Jack and hopefully someday there would be more between us. I wanted more, but I needed to hear Jack tell me he loved me. Why were those words so important to me? Because I never heard them in any aspect of my life…and I craved to be loved.

Christmas came early and I awoke with eyes swollen from crying myself to sleep the night before. I heard Mother's "Merry Christmas" and glanced at the clock. Two a.m. It never failed. Mother was obsessed with getting up early every year.

I dragged myself out of bed and into the bathroom. I splashed water on my face, hoping to bring some resemblance of myself without giving my tears away. Finally satisfied that I just looked tired, I stumbled out of the bathroom.

Christmas was the one time of year that I felt the most at home here in my family. There weren't snide comments, no digs that made me feel worthless. Christmas seemed to bring everyone into a happier light, at least for the day. We opened presents and I gushed over clothes I had picked out and my parents had wrapped. We all laughed at how good I had become at faking being surprised. If only they realized how good I had become at faking life. They apparently were oblivious to the fact that I was simply going through the motions on a daily basis – except when I was with Jack. Those moments I truly felt like myself.

I showered and put my presents in my bedroom to prepare for round two of Christmas. Breakfast and presents with my grandparents on my mother's side. This was my favorite part of Christmas. My grandparents adored me and I could talk to my grandmother like no one else. There was no judgement from her, and she just listened and told me it would be alright. I would find my way and when I did my grandmother promised me she would be right there next to me cheering me on. The love I had from my grandparents was one of pure unconditional love, the way it was supposed to be.

I was at the door when my grandparents arrived. Papa folded me into his arms and kissed my forehead. "How's my Izzy?"

"I'm good, Papa." I held him close and inhaled the scent of his pipe. I loved the smell of that old pipe.

"Now, now, let that girl get to me." Gram pushed through the door and pulled me from Grandfather's arms and into hers.

I giggled. "Love you, Gram."

I linked an arm through my grandparents' and we made our way to the living room. For the moment, the cloud of despair left me and I found myself glowing in the affection and attention from Gram and Papa. After we had opened presents, my parents went to the kitchen to cook breakfast. This was the time I loved. I had a moment to just talk with my grandparents.

"Well, tell me all about him." Gram sat close on the couch next to me.

"What did you hear?"

"Oh, your mother just said some boy was wanting to date you."

"Oh, Gram, we *are* dating. He's so cute. Wait till you see him." I paused. "Gram, how do you know if you love someone?"

Gram leaned in and whispered, "You just know."

I shook my head. "But how? And how long does it take to fall in love?"

The couch cushion sank next to me as Papa flanked my other side. "Izzy, sometimes all it takes is a second. That first glance and you're a goner. That's what happened when I saw your grandmother. First sight and I knew I was going to marry that woman."

My eyes teared up. "I'm afraid I'm going to miss it when it happens and I won't know."

They both wrapped their arms around me. "You'll know. Listen to your heart. It won't steer you wrong."

I whispered, "I hope not."

five

I awoke Saturday morning and laid in bed mentally going through the clothes in my closet. What was I going to wear? Jack was taking me to the base to show me around. Would I see any of his superiors? My stomach clenched in anticipation. What kind of impression would I make if I did meet people he worked with? Or would it be quiet and we could just enjoy each other?

I pulled myself from the bed and headed for the shower. The hot water ran over me, washing away any apprehension about the day. I thought of my grandparents and the love they shared at such a quick time frame in meeting each other. I often wondered if I had the ability to love, or would that just pass me by where I would go through life alone. One never really knows what can be expected from life, but one thing was for sure, in the past month the thoughts of suicide and my attempt were thought of less and less as my thoughts were filled with Jack.

Dressed in jeans, sneakers and a mint green sweater, I patiently applied two coats of mascara to my eyelashes. That was all the make-up I was going to put on today. Jack had told me repeatedly he liked me with no make-up, the natural look. He spoke of me having a natural beauty. I often balked at hearing it, but he would hold me gently by the cheeks and say "really hear the words".

I was just putting away the mascara and straightening my room when Mother appeared in the doorway. "I'm not happy at today, Isabelle. I only hope that you will remember things I have said and behave yourself. No man will be with a girl long term who is easy."

I sighed. "I'm not easy, Mom. And Jack isn't like that."

"You shouldn't be going to the base."

"Mom, he's showing me around base. We're not going to his barracks."

Mother nodded. "I hope not. I would be extremely disappointed in you if you did."

"I get it, okay. You don't want me to do anything that will shame you or dad." I walked by her and hoped Jack arrived soon. I needed out of this house.

The knock on the door was serendipity as I walked into the living room. I hurried to the door. "Let me just grab my coat."

Jack stepped inside and waited. I took in the bomber jacket over a button down shirt with jeans. Suddenly I was shy, until those blue eyes met mine.

Mother came into the room. "I hope you two will behave yourselves." Her pointed statement was a direct hit to Jack.

"Yes, ma'am. We wouldn't dream of not behaving."

Mother nodded, yet the disapproval was overwhelming.

"Let's go." I appeared at Jack's side with my coat on.

Jack and I rode in silence, as had become our custom, for most of the way to the base. We held hands and I sat close to him, my head on his shoulder. I loved riding like this. We didn't have to speak, but simply be with each other and there was a conversation between us that only we seemed to understand.

As we arrived on base, Jack immediately started pointing out things as we drove around. His place of work, where he ate, shopped...the pride rang through as he described everything to me. We drove down the street where the married housing was. I let myself imagine being there with Jack, having a family.

"Someday, I hope my family will be there for me as I continue my military career." The wistfulness in his voice surprised me.

"Why wouldn't they?" I asked.

"I mean my future family--wife, kids..." He trailed off as he glanced at the housing we were passing. Were we thinking the same thing? Could he imagine me beside him or was he thinking of someone he had yet to meet?

"You want to make the Air Force a career?" I turned to him. Jack rarely talked about work.

"I do want to, but it's not easy for the family. There's always a chance of deployment and always the danger of a short life expectancy." He shrugged. "I realize there aren't a lot of women that would be able to handle that...so maybe making this my career won't be the way it ends up."

"I think if you marry the right person, they would follow you to the end of the earth so you can follow your dreams." I'd follow him, but I didn't want to say that. Jack was still unreadable as to his feelings for me. I know it had only been a few weeks, but I couldn't tell how he felt.

"Maybe." Jack flashed that smile that made my insides melt every time. I kept my eyes on Jack as he drove along. This man with a quiet demeanor had dreams that I imagined he didn't share often. He wanted what everyone at our age did, I supposed, someone to love and be supportive of his hopes and dreams and share them with him. It was a comfort to me to think he may have some uncertainty about the future as I did. Maybe I wasn't so different in my thinking like I had thought.

He then pulled up in front of his barracks and parked the car. "Do you want to come in and see my room?"

I nodded. My stomach flipped and I knew it wasn't nerves, yet anticipation of seeing where he slept, thought of me. We wandered through the barracks hand in hand as he pointed things out and finally reached his room. He opened the door and allowed me to step inside. It was nothing special, just an ordinary room, yet I felt overwhelmed in the space.

As I took off my coat and sat down on the edge of the bed, I looked around. Before I knew it, Jack was standing in front of me. He leaned down and kissed me gently, leaning me backward onto the bed. I pulled him down on top of me, and I could feel the bulge of him through his jeans.

My heart quickened.

The kiss deepened, and I stroked his tongue with mine. This was all so foreign, yet natural at the same time. I didn't dare tell him I was a virgin, fearing he would stop.

Jack fumbled as he pulled my sweater off and released me from my bra. His mouth closed upon one of my nipples. I shut my eyes and willed myself to relax. I wanted him so badly, but I didn't know how he felt. Did he want this as much as me? Or was it just the guy thing to do? I tugged at his shirt and pulled it over his head, forcing us to move apart for just the moment.

He looked down at me and smiled. He unbuttoned my jeans and tugged them, as well as my underwear off my hips and removed them in unison. I laid there watching him as he removed the rest of his clothing before coming back to me. I pulled him close as our kiss deepened. I ran my hands along his back, marveling at the feel of his muscles and the way they moved as he moved against me. He pulled back and looked into my eyes as he pushed forward into me.

An unexpected discomfort hit me and I bit my lip.

Jack froze, a look of horror crossing his face.

"Isabelle, why didn't you say something?" He pulled from me and stood up, backing away. I sat up and watched him.

"Please, Jack. I don't want you to stop."

"I would have done this different had I known." He ran his fingers through his hair and sighed. He sat down beside me and held me close. I wanted to cry. Just like that he had no desire for me.

"Isabelle, look at me."

I swallowed hard and blinked the tears away as I looked up at him. "Jack…"

"I don't want to hurt you. What do you want?"

"I want you, Jack. Please." The simple words had him gathering me into his arms and rolling me onto the bed until I was on my back and he was atop of me.

"Are you sure?" Jack whispered the words against my throat as he kissed me.

"Yes, oh, god, yes." I moved against him, thrilled at the feel of his hardness against me. He did desire me and I needed to be desired, *needed* to be loved.

I moved in time with him. Our kisses bringing us closer and closer if that was possible with the way we were already connected, him deep inside of me. I relished in the thought of his act of love and I couldn't have been happier at the only gift I could give him that he would receive it so willingly.

As he gave his final thrust, I held him close to me, our hearts in unison with their beating. He breathed heavy into my ear. After a moment, he rolled off me and pulled me with him as he moved onto his back. I closed my eyes with my head laying on his chest. The beating of his heart lulled me into a sense of security. No words of love were spoken, but I finally knew without a doubt this was the man I loved. It wasn't because of the act of sex we had just shared, but it was the way he reacted with gentleness and caring. This man had held my heart since the moment I spied those dimples and blue eyes, and although I hadn't realized it at the time, I knew at this moment laying here in his arms, listening to his heart that his heartbeat would forever be my lifeline.

There were no words between us. None were needed. Jack's hand roamed slowly up and down my arm, keeping the warmth between us strong. I snuggled closer, if that was possible, and he chuckled. He reached down and grabbed a blanket and pulled it up over us.

"Cold?"

"No, I just can't get close enough to you." I ran my hand along his chest. *How could I have gotten so lucky?*

"Were we not closer just a minute ago?" He kissed my forehead and pulled me tight to him.

"Yes, but that was a minute ago and I'm already missing you." The words flowed so easily out of my mouth. I closed my eyes tight. The day couldn't end, please...I needed this moment to last forever.

We laid in each other's arms, holding on tightly to each other and the moment we shared for what seemed like hours. I knew as the shadows grew in the room that we would need to be leaving soon. I got up to use the bathroom. Upon returning, Jack was fully dressed again, straightening his bed. I grabbed my clothes and dressed as quickly as I could. The moment was over. Unsureness washed over me and I glanced at Jack to see if I could read him.

He walked over to me, a grin upon his face. He wrapped his arms around me and kissed me gently, his tongue teasing me. "Oh, Isabelle. I don't want to take you home."

I smiled. The unsureness rolled off me and I hugged him close. "I don't want today to end."

We rode in silence the hour drive back to the house. I was nestled up against him. Thoughts of the suicide attempt ran through my mind and I knew I had to tell him. For once, I really wanted to talk about it. But something held me back. What was he feeling? I still couldn't tell if he had just wanted sex or did he truly care for me? It didn't matter. The precious gift I gave to him I had given freely and without reservation. What he did with it at this point was up to him.

"Are you okay? Sore?"

I lifted my head from his shoulder. "I'm fine. Better than fine."

He smiled down at me. "I didn't know, Isabelle."

I nodded. "I know. But it was what I wanted."

He brought my hand to his lips and kissed it. "Maybe we need to talk about it…what you've given me isn't to be taken lightly. There's an obligation with it."

I stiffened. *No, please don't feel obligated towards me.* He kissed my hand again.

"It wasn't given lightly. Nothing more to discuss." I heard the words as they came out of my mouth and felt the wall going back up. I wanted love not a marriage proposal out of obligation because I lost my virginity to him. We rode the rest of the way in silence, each obviously consumed by our own thoughts. I couldn't bear to think of what Jack was thinking. I wanted a declaration of love. I needed to feel wanted and desired, not just for sex, but for me as a whole. My mind, my body and all the emotion that raged inside of me.

I bit my tongue, wanting to spill everything out – my past, the present and what I wanted for the future – everything that included him. I couldn't. He would walk away from me if he knew about the suicide attempt. My only chance at really finding happiness was to lock that part of me away and never talk about it again.

I kissed Jack before getting out of the car, holding him close, listening to his heart beat once more for a brief second.

"Are you sure you're okay?" He whispered the words against my hair as he pulled me closer.

"I am." I held back the words *I love you* and gave him a tender kiss that I hoped he would see through to the love I was feeling. He walked me to the door and kissed me once again before leaving.

I watched the taillights fade from sight as he drove down the road before I took a deep breath and stepped inside. My parents were in the living room waiting for me.

"Well, you're later than we expected." Mother's words hit me. Every bit of happiness I had felt that day melted away and I was left with a darkness of despair.

"We didn't say a time and it's not that late." I looked at the clock. Six.

"I assumed you wouldn't be gone all day and that you would understand that was the expectation." Mother looked at me expectantly. I knew that you-owe-me-an-apology look. I squared my shoulders and stared at my mother. "Don't look at me that way."

I shrugged. "I'll be in my room, as always."

I shut the door quietly behind me and sank to the floor with my back against it. I couldn't do it. The moment of happiness and hope that I had when I was with Jack was never going to change my life, my family life. I was destined to be unhappy forever and to live in this perpetual state of disillusionment with life. My heart ached for his touch and for his warmth. I could feel his heartbeat still, but my own had gone silent and was no longer beating in sync to his. I knew in the very depths of my soul what I had to do and it broke my heart. Why? Why couldn't I just have more time?

six

Sunday morning came and I told my mother I was sick and couldn't go to church. I fell back into a fitful sleep trying to change the outcome of my life in every dream I had. The phone rang and I ignored it. I wasn't about to get out of bed, although I knew it wouldn't be Jack. He would be sitting in church wondering where I was.

Dragging myself from the bed, I jumped in the hot shower and stood there trying to make sense of the path I was about to embark on. The water rained over me and my mind did not clear with the steam, instead I was more confused than ever as I shut the water off and dried off. Dressing for warmth, I started for the living room to grab my boots. I longed to get into the fresh air and go for a walk. Just as I was slipping into my coat, my parents walked through the door...with Jack.

"Oh, you are up." Mother shot me a glance that silenced me from speaking.

"I was going to go for a walk." I glanced at Jack.

"Good. I'll go with you." Jack gestured for me to proceed him out the door.

We walked in silence until we were out of the driveway and some ways down the road. Jack then reached for my hand and I reluctantly pulled it from my pocket and allowed him to hold my hand. The warmth shocked me. It was no different than any other time, but this time I was cold inside and out.

"Isabelle…" Jack started and stopped. He glanced at me and looked away. "Talk to me, please."

I looked up at him and stopped walking. Jack stopped next to me. I searched his face for some sort of clue of how he was feeling. All I saw was confusion on his face. There was no flash of the dimples and his blue eyes were filled with hurt. I sighed. "I don't know what to say. What did I do?"

I wrapped my arms around him. "Nothing. You've been perfect. It's not you, I promise." I relented and softened towards him and once again was aware of our hearts being in sync. I needed this, needed him. And my heart ached with the thought of what was to come.

"Isabelle, I think we need to talk about yesterday. I didn't want to hurt you."

"You didn't hurt me. I told you, I wanted it too." I looked at him and the hurt had cleared from those blue eyes. "I was afraid to tell you before that I had never…I thought you wouldn't want me."

Jack pulled me close. "I want you, always. Isabelle, please believe me when I say I only stopped because I didn't want to hurt you. I would have done things so differently if I had known. You deserved better than that."

I smiled. "Come on." We continued walking, holding

hands. The silence was no longer stagnant and awkward. We were beating in time again.

"Is there something more?" Jack spoke breaking the silence.

"What do you mean?" I glanced up at him.

"I just feel like you pull away sometimes. What happens to make you do that? Have I done something beyond the other day at the barracks that makes you uncomfortable?"

I didn't know how to verbalize what I was feeling. I shook my head.

"Talk to me, please." Jack's voice was soft, but when I looked at him, his eyes were filled of compassion.

"We've talked about how I don't fit into my family, Jack."

"What else?" Jack stopped me and turned to face me. "What is it that you're not telling me?"

I closed my eyes and took a deep breath. I couldn't tell him about the suicide attempt. "It's just every time I'm with you, I'm happy...content for probably the first time in my life." I paused. "But then *she* finds some way to take that away from me. In an instant after we are apart, she has me feeling so worthless and unloved."

"Izzy, you're loved." Jack pulled me close, wrapping his arms around me, enfolding me into his warmth--a security that I found myself relaxing into. I wondered if he meant he loved me or if truly thought my parents loved me.

We walked until we were starting to get cold and then turned around and walked back to the house. By the time we arrived, we were bone cold and in desperate need of some hot chocolate. Jack followed me into the house and as we took off jackets and boots, I took them to the closet. Jack followed me into the kitchen and watched as I put the kettle on the stove to heat the water.

I pulled two mugs from the cupboard and scooped hot chocolate mix into them. I glanced over to him and those dimples flashed at me. I walked over to him and stood on tippy-toes to give him a quick kiss. I danced out of his reach as he tried to enclose me in his arms. The kettle whistled as the steam escaped the spout. I took it off the heat and poured the hot water over the chocolate in the mugs. I set the kettle down and felt Jack's presence behind me. He wasn't quite touching me, but the heat from him pulled me in and I leaned back to find his rock-hard chest right there to catch me. He nuzzled my neck and I closed my eyes to enjoy the feel of his mouth on me.

"Ready?" Jack's voice was muffled by his mouth against my skin.

"For?" My voice trembled.

"Hot chocolate, of course." He chuckled as I groaned. "This is your parents' house, for God's sake, have some control." His voice was almost too soft to hear, but I caught the words and tried not to laugh out loud. I stirred our cocoa and handed him the mug.

"Fire's going." I nodded towards the living room. We settled onto the floor in front of the fireplace sipping our drinks. The heat soon seeped into our bodies, although was it from the fireplace, or the playfulness that had ensued in the kitchen, I was unsure. I watched Jack carefully, wishing I could read his mind. Sitting side by side, his fingers found mine and although barely touching, I felt his strength. I was dying to know what he was thinking, but judging from his relaxed mode, he was content with my presence as I was with his.

seven

New Year's Eve was here. Jack had to stay on base so I sat at home like usual preparing to watch the ball drop by myself at midnight. It was another year and nothing had changed. Well, not true. I had found love, but here I was alone once again on a night that was supposed to commemorate the ending of the old and the starting of the new.

As the past few days has gone by since our time at base, I had flourished in my newfound love for Jack. Although I still didn't know how he felt, he was there with me when he could be and he gave all appearances of truly caring for me. But those three little words I longed to hear were elusive and I held back saying them myself. There was nothing worse than saying them only to find out the love wasn't reciprocated.

I glanced down at the paper I held in my hand. It was almost midnight and Jack had given me the number of the pay phone on his floor in the barracks. I picked up the phone and dialed the number. Jack picked up on the second ring.

"What's the time?"

Isabelle laughed. "We have two minutes. I wish you could see the ball drop like I can, or better yet that you were sitting here with me."

I heard the sigh come through the phone. "Me too, Izzy, me too." It was the first time he called me Izzy and I grew warm.

"Ready…the clock is coming on at the bottom of the TV. Ten, nine, eight, seven, six, five, four, three, two, one, Happy New Year." Isabelle spoke the last three words just as Jack did.

"Happy New Year, my Izzy." He said it again.

"You too, Jack. I…" I stopped myself. I couldn't.

"You what?" Jack questioned.

"I can't wait to see you." The words sounded lame as I said them and I wished more than anything I could be brave and just tell him I loved him, heart and soul. We signed off.

New Year's had come and gone. I felt no comfort in my decision. The thought of what I had to do made my chest tighten in anxiety. I had tried to play out different scenarios. It didn't matter what I did…someone was about to get hurt, and all around I was the one who ended up with a shattered heart. It was a dreary day at the start of January. I decided to tag along with Mother to go to the mall on the coast. I had gotten some money for Christmas and it would be a good time to spend it.

Jack and I had talked very few times since that fateful day in December, one that I would never forget. I relived that moment in my mind daily. It had been the happiest day of my life. The love I felt for Jack grew with each minute. I missed his touch, his voice when we didn't talk.

But in those times when we weren't talking, there was snide comments and remarks at how thankful things were back to normal. Did my mother think I could forget Jack's touch, his kiss, his dimples, his blue eyes? She was delusional if she thought I was going to be any happier with a life sitting here at home, being torn down daily. I'd had enough and needed to take action.

So today was a day of therapeutic shopping hopefully, some retail therapy. My mother and I parted ways once we got to the mall. Mother was on a mission for some very specific household items that I care nothing about and I had some clothes I wanted to look for. I wandered from store to store without any real luck. I didn't really see what was in the store. This was the mall Jack and I walked, hand in hand. I saw him at every turn.

Finally parking myself on a bench to just wait for mother, I peopled watched. So many happy couples strolling by, hand in hand, laughing and talking, all of them bursting at the seams with happiness. I glanced up further down the mall and blinked. Jack was strolling towards me. Once I caught his eye, those dimples flashed. My inside quivered. God, if he wasn't the most handsome man alive.

He leaned down and kissed me before sliding on to the bench next to me. I took a deep breath.

"I called your house. Your dad said you were here."

"Oh." I knew in my heart I had to let this man go before I fell too far in love with him. I glanced over at him and he was watching me, a look of bewilderment on his face.

"What's going on, Izzy?" He reached for my hand, yet his body stiffened next to me.

I didn't want to pull my hand away, but the warmth of his touch was weakening my resolve. "Nothing."

Yeah, one-word answers were the way to go. I needed him to walk away. I couldn't tell him I loved him, and I didn't think he loved me. I looked everywhere around me but at Jack. I couldn't face those blue eyes and the hurt in them.

"Talk to me. Did you have another fight with your mother?" I heard the anguish in his voice, yet he leaned in towards me. Although next to me, he angled his body to face me. I could feel Jack's eyes staring at me and I wanted to fall into his arms and tell him everything. He was going to walk away anyway if he ever found out about the suicide attempt. I couldn't put that burden on him. I just hoped someday he would forgive me and realize that I saved him from the misery I was feeling.

"It's nothing." The words were cold and dismissing. But then I made a fatal mistake and turned to look at him. Those blue eyes stared at me, wide and full of hurt. The pain in his eyes pierced my heart. It was a physical pain like I had never felt before. A knife to the heart and twisted hard. It took my breath away and I longed to take back the words. Instead Jack stood and stared at me for a moment. He opened his mouth to speak, but shook his head before turning and walking away.

I watched him go. My heart shattered into a thousand pieces with each step he took further from me. My vision became cloudy as tears filled my eyes. *Please, come back. Fight for me. Tell me you love me.* I watched him walk further and further away. In my twisted logic, I had just saved him from the mess I was, but in my own body, I was broken and would never be the same.

"Was that Jack?" Mother's voice came from behind me. I blinked tears away before turning around.

"Yes."

Mother watched me. I gestured to her bags. "Find everything you were looking for."

"Yes. Are you coming home with me?" Mother looked down the mall aisle, but Jack was nowhere to be seen.

"Of course."

"You don't want to spend time with Jack?" Mother asked.

I wanted to scream at her *No, you got what you wanted*. I simply shook my head. I was fighting to keep the tears from flowing, but I couldn't be weak. I had made my choice and made sure that he walked away. I had to live with the memory of the hurt coming from his eyes, the blue eyes that had first mesmerized me. I would never forgive myself for the pain I had caused him. But if you love someone, they tell you to let them go. And he wasn't coming back so, in my nonsensical logic, that was a pretty sure sign he never loved me.

And of course, my mother was right. I didn't deserve to be happy after all I had done to ruin not only my own life, but everyone else's around me also. I wanted to scream in frustration. Being in love wasn't supposed to hurt like this. My grandmother had made it sound like something wonderful. Maybe it was just me...I wasn't made for love or to have that happily ever after that they tell young girls they will have once they meet the man of their dreams. Maybe I was destined to be alone the rest of my life, content with my memories of Jack and the one day we shared that forever changed my life. He had allowed me to open my heart to him, even if I hadn't communicated it and that was the gift I needed from him. He gave me the one opportunity to experience love in its raw and vulnerable state, a place in which I couldn't handle because I was defective, broken and never to be repaired.

Once back home, I escaped to my room. There was no explaining the past five weeks and how I had such a connection with Jack. My chest hurt and I wondered if I was having a heart attack. I sat on the floor in my room, knees to my chest with my arms wrapped around my legs. I rested my head on my knees and just sat there. I built the wall around my heart with every memory, trying to shut out the emotional pain and the physical pain I was feeling. I longed for the numbness of depression to overtake me and allow me to feel nothing. Instead I felt love for Jack, and sorrow for myself at the way I treated him. He didn't deserve that. And it wasn't intentional to hurt him. I wanted to save him from me, because I did love him.

I was so messed up. I stayed in my room, listening to music that matched my sorrow. My mind found constantly, day by day and sometimes minute by minute, to fight the blackness that threatened to consume me. I had been fighting this since I was a young girl. Never happy, never fitting in to my own family. Barely making it through high school and then trying to end it all, and *failing* once again. I barely could force myself out of bed and would only escape to the shower so I wouldn't hear my mother's voice. I ate the bare minimum that kept my parents from asking questions, but food churned my stomach and threaten to send anything I ate right back up.

Jack had been a lifeline for me these past five weeks. Giving me hope, the sense of the possibility that I might make it through the darkness after all. All I wanted was to hear him say those words...I love you...words to assure me that what I *felt* in his touch was real. Did I imagine his tender touch, his gestures of kindness and love when he held me after I had a fight with my mother? I knew there was love in his touch, why did I need to hear the words? Was I that insecure? Why could I not accept what he gave me and let it go at that? Why need more? Maybe life wasn't meant to give us more. There seemed to be no rhyme or reason as to who found happiness and who didn't.

I closed my eyes and allowed myself the memory of that day, December 28, a day that would forever be imprinted in my mind. Jack had been so tender and gentle. I longed to lay in his arms again and feel his strength. I could see the barracks, his room, us laying on the bed in the aftermath. His heartbeat I felt against my own.

Tears streamed down my face as I tried to hold back, but I was caught up in the memory and the sorrow of losing the one man I loved. The one man I had found happiness with, joy for the first time in my life. And I forced him to walk away. Now that's a special kind of messed up. I cried until there were no more tears, just a hole in my heart and the ensuing pain that came with it.

I dragged myself from the floor and crawled into bed. It was early, although dark outside because of the winter hours. Fully clothed, I pulled the blanket up over me and willed myself to feel him next to me. I wasn't sure when I drifted off to sleep, but when I awoke it was fully dark. I glanced over to the clock to see the time of three a.m.

Getting out of bed, I used the bathroom and made my way to the kitchen to make a sandwich. I wanted to scream in the silence of the house. Instead I made a sandwich and ate it almost robotically as I sat in a trance. My heart still ached and I was so desperate for someone

– *anyone* -- to talk to. Even my mother. Someone who would tell me it would be alright and tell me to call him, apologize and fight to get him back.

As much as I knew my grandparents would be supportive, I felt such a burden that I would disappoint them that I couldn't bring myself to talk to them about Jack. Gram had asked me to dinner and I had refused, knowing her and Papa would ask about him.

My heavy heart brought me back to the present. I couldn't fight for him. I couldn't admit to him I had made a mistake. He would never forgive me for the hurt I caused. I had forced him to walk away and it was something I had to live with. The desire to call him and apologize, beg him for forgiveness was overwhelming. I forced myself to stay in my room, away from the telephone, to stop any foolishness of impulsively calling him. My body ached from the wrenching sobs that shook through me. I prayed for the darkness to overtake me and let me escape the pain.

The next couple of weeks went by in a blur and I went through the motions at work and at home. I wanted to scream for someone to ask me about Jack. But it was like he had never existed. My parents never mentioned him, never asked why he didn't call or come around anymore. It was like the couple of months he was in my life never existed. Had it been a dream?

My dreams were filled with Jack. Not a night didn't go by that I didn't cry myself to sleep over the loss. It wasn't just him being gone, it was the loss of the opportunities that could have been, the what if's in life that I rolled through in my mind like a movie. I wondered how many tears I would cry over this man. I felt as if I couldn't cry another one, and yet they fell night after night.

eight

I found myself evolving as the months rolled by. Winter had moved to spring and now as the summer approach, I found myself longing to move. Run from the memories and my past. Tears still fell every night, but I had found a way to numb the pain. I wasn't sure how I did it, but I cried for Jack and the lost opportunities between us, but I hardened my heart to the piercing pain that came. The physical pain came less frequent now and I held on to thoughts of running away from everything I once knew to start over.

Using the work computers after hours, I put together a plan. I found some rental properties in Virginia along the coast that were doable. I started submitting resumes to jobs in the area using my work email address. I had cleared it with my boss and he knew I was looking to move out of State. He didn't know the reasons, as I had put on quite the show stating I was just needing to find some place that could give me more. He knew nothing of my past and I kept it that way. The past was a thing to forget. I didn't want to think of all the mistakes I had already made at my tender age of eighteen, soon to be nineteen. I felt a lot older and contributed it to having an "old soul".

My parents had never spoken of Jack again after that day in the mall. Mother acted like we were the perfect family. I had never done anything to bring attention to the dysfunction in the family, and I had never fallen in love. My mother's ability to act like an ostrich was uncanny.

I just couldn't do it anymore.

And then one morning it happened, I had three emails with request for interviews. I reviewed each one and replied I could be in the area for an interview in three weeks. They all answered me within a couple of hours. After clearing it with my boss, I booked flights and a hotel room. I had three interviews set for one day and I would be able to look around the area for an apartment. I hoped it would go smoothly and soon I would be able to move on.

I told my parents a small white lie that I had to go to Virginia on a business trip. I stated my boss was taking a case that required him to talk to some people down there and I would be flying down with him to take notes. It sounded plausible and my parents, although not happy that I would be traveling, didn't say much. What could they say? This was for my job.

I was excited and petrified at the same time. Almost paralyzed with fear, I sat in the airport waiting for my flight wondering what the hell I was doing. And then sat there thinking if Jack would work in an airport like this, following his dream of being an air traffic controller.

Would he stay in the Air Force for a career or would he choose to get out early and go work in the private sector?

I found myself holding on to the familiar ache in my chest that I had every time I thought of him. It was like my heart was still reaching out to him, looking for its match to beat in time with. And yet the reminder of what I had done, the hurt in his eyes, pushed me to find my confidence to nail these job interviews and start my life over. I was determined if I changed jobs and location that I would be able to forget the past. Little did I know that you can't outrun the past, it follows you everywhere you go.

Coming from small town in New Hampshire, I was a bit overwhelmed as I deplaned at Norfolk International Airport. I had never traveled out of New Hampshire before. Thankful I had only a carry on with me and didn't need to find the baggage claim, and headed for the rental cars. My boss had helped me secure everything I needed to be down here and had mapped out for me the route I needed to take from airport to my hotel and to my interviews. Although the airport was only fifteen miles to Hampton, Virginia where all three of my interviews were, I was nervous about driving having never been in the area.

Navigating through the traffic wasn't bad and I found myself relaxing and actually enjoying the scenery. Although it was only the end of May, the weather was gorgeous and warm enough that I drove with the windows down. Finally checked in to my hotel, I decided to drive around to where my interviews were so I would have an idea where to go in the morning. I had been smart to arrive in Virginia on Sunday night for Monday interviews. Traffic had been fairly light and it gave me the chance to explore without having to deal with a ton of traffic. I drove by the offices and started scouting around for apartments.

The hotel clerk had been nice enough to get me a paper from that morning so I could look at rental listings. There were quite a few in the area, although pricey, depending on what I could get paid for a job, I might be able to swing a studio apartment. After all, it was just me and I didn't need a lot of space. And lucky me, there were even furnished ones available that would help me to get started having no furniture to bring along.

The waiting room of my first interview was tastefully decorated and had a peaceful quality to it. The beige stuffed chairs were laid out in an asymmetrical way to give the appearance of home. After checking in, I sank into a nearby chair and took in the surroundings. The various posters of book covers spoke of the number of authors Bookend Publishing represented, but they were also numerous bestsellers scattered around.

My heart raced with the anticipation of meeting the infamous senior editor, Gayle Sutherland. I had been a big fan of her work in the various authors I had read. My research revealed how she was a stickler for perfection and demanded no less from her authors that she worked with. She put in long hours and demanded her employees do the same. When I saw the ad for an editorial administrator working directly with her I jumped at the chance and immediately forwarded my resume. It hadn't been a few days before I had a reply and they were eager to work with me in setting up the interview so I could do it while I was here for the other two I had planned.

This was my first choice of a job here in Virginia, and I wanted this to go well. My palms were sticky with sweat, nerves frazzled.

"Isabelle." I stood and faced the receptionist. She gestured down the hall. "First door on the left. Ms. Sutherland is ready for you."

Nodding my thanks, I proceeded down the hall. The door was open, and I knocked with confidence.

"Isabelle, come on it." Gayle Sutherland stood as I approached the desk, reaching out her right hand.

"Thank you for seeing me." I shook her hand and sat down in the chair across from her.

"Tell me a little bit about yourself." She sat back, eyes on me intently.

"Well, I am looking to relocate to this area. I have secretarial experience in a law firm, and although I know it is not the publishing industry, I feel I would be a great fit for your team. I've read numerous of your authors that you personally work with and this is a field I would like to learn more about and make my way up the ladder to one day work beside you."

"That's ambitious. You worked for a law firm. Did they specialize in industry contracts?"

"There was a lawyer there that did, yes, however I was not working with him. I was working as an administrator for a family law attorney."

Gayle nodded. She jotted a few notes down and sat back. "You realize you don't have much experience, actually no experience in this field."

"I do. However, I am a quick learner and will put in whatever hours it takes to learn and master the business." I sat forward. "I just need you to take a chance on me."

"That's quite a lot you are asking of me...to take a leap of faith and take a chance on someone I don't know, isn't personally referred to me by someone I trust and someone who could move here and then be homesick and leave in short order."

"That's true. The only guarantee I can give you is that there is nothing in New Hampshire holding me there and homesickness won't be an issue. I can also guarantee you that I will put 120% into everything I do. I'm single and a loner. Long hours are not an issue for me." I crossed my legs, praying I exuded the confidence I so desperately wanted to convey.

Ms. Sutherland leaned back in her chair, lacing her fingers together to hold them to her lips. Her eyes never strayed from mine and I was praying I could hold the eye contact. She nodded. "Well, let's give you a tour of the place and see what you think of it. You may have second thoughts after seeing behind the scenes."

I followed her around the building; she was quite thorough on the tour. We stood and watched a brainstorming session with the art department on a cover. "You would be expected to sit in on these sessions for my authors. We have final say on the cover as the editor."

I nodded. I took it all in, although it was a bit overwhelming, I couldn't help but feel the excitement build within me. I needed this job. This would be the beginning of the new me. We wrapped up the tour near the door to the reception area.

Gayle nodded again. "When do you leave to go back to New Hampshire?"

"I leave Wednesday. That will give me tomorrow and Tuesday to look around at apartments."

"Okay, then. Why don't you plan on coming back tomorrow, eight a.m. sharp, and you can shadow me for the day. I'll make a decision by tomorrow afternoon."

"Thank you. I will see you then." I shook her hand again and left. I held my composure until I got out to the parking lot and slid into my car. My hands shook. I just might have a chance at this job. I glanced at my watched. This interview had taken longer than I expected and I had about fifteen minutes to get to the next one. The other two now were just something I needed to get done, as this job was the one I truly wanted.

The other two interviews were short and sweet. I felt good about them, however, they didn't interest me like working with Gayle Sutherland did. I was finished with all interviews by one in the afternoon. I headed back to the hotel to change and decided to go take a walk on the beach. After all, this could be the only chance I had if none of these jobs panned out.

The warm sand immediately put me at ease. I had kicked off the flip flops as soon as I stepped foot onto the beach. I walked slowly through the soft sand, enjoying the heat radiating through my feet, making my way to the packed sand closer to the water's edge. It was still cool in Virginia, but I was going to feel that ocean even if it was just for a second. I stopped at the edge and let the waves lap my feet as they came in and out. Although a cool contrast to the warm sand, I closed my eyes and enjoyed the stress-free zone. No matter what happened, this is where I wanted to be. If I had to run away from life, this is where I was running to.

I could picture my life here. Watching the sunrise over the ocean every morning, walking the beach at night after a long day at work. I didn't care what I time I got out of work, if I lived close enough I would feel the sand between my toes every night, rain or shine. I turned around and looked across the street. Apartment buildings lined up. That was my first place to look for a place to live, preferably one whose balcony overlooked the ocean.

With a plan in mind, I started for the apartment buildings. Hopefully the leasing office would be open and there would be openings. I wouldn't be able to rent one without confirmation that a job had been offered, but I could at least start looking.

nine

I stood on the balcony of my hotel room watching the sunrise over the ocean. I inhaled deeply and exhaled as I watched the waves roll in and out over the sand. Sleep had eluded me last night as I ran through different scenarios of how today would go at the publishing house. No matter how much I tried, I could not speed up time. Watching the ocean calmed those nerves a bit. Although my stomach churned, I knew I had to get at least some toast into it if I was going to make it through the day.

Glancing at my watch, noting it was seven a.m., I slipped my bare feet into a pair of gray pumps to match my blue and gray striped sheath dress. I scrutinized myself in the mirror and decided I looked professional and ready to take on this new world, even if I didn't quite feel it. Fake it till you make it. I gave myself a mental thumbs up and headed downstairs to grab a quick breakfast before driving the fifteen minutes to Bookend Publishing.

I arrived at Bookend Publishing at quarter of eight. Fifteen minutes early. In my mind that was sharp. I made my way into the reception area and checked in. The receptionist smiled warmly. "Ms. Sutherland is waiting for you in her office."

The door was open and I knocked. Gayle never looked up, but gestured for me to enter. As I got closer, I realized she had a Bluetooth ear piece in and was listening to something on the phone. I sat down silently and waited.

Gayle ended the call. "Ready?"

I pulled out a notebook from my purse and nodded. She smiled. "You can leave your purse here, but bring the notebook and pen. We've got meetings this morning."

She was on the move and I dropped my purse in front of her desk and hustled to keep up with her. The first stop was a marketing meeting. I took simple notes outlining the gist of the meeting so I would know what to expect the next time—hopefully there would be a next time. The discussion centered around Gayle's new author's debut release. It was expected to do well and they wanted to really push the marketing. I was surprised when Gayle pulled back a bit on some of the plans, stating the author needed to prove herself first.

Next stop was a meeting with the cover art department. Three different mock ups were up on easels as we entered the room. Gayle wandered between the three, staring at each of them and not saying a word. Others present in the room sat at the table just waiting for her to speak. I focused on the mock ups and studied each one in depth, comparing them to the next one. In my mind, there was one clear one that stood out as the best depiction of the story, from what I had read with the back-cover copy.

"Well, Isabelle, what do you think?" Gayle stepped back away from the mock ups. Praying this was a test I could pass, I moved to be in front of the three. I took them all in again, and turned to Gayle.

"The middle one, no doubt, in my opinion, is the best choice."

"Really? Why would you say the best choice?"

"Well, I haven't read the book, but after reading the back-cover copy, this cover definitely depicts the storyline the best and it is the one my eyes gravitated towards as soon as we entered the room."

Gayle nodded as I spoke. "Good eye." She turned towards the waiting group and simple announced "that's the one".

As we walked down the hall to the next meeting, Gayle put her hand on my arm and stopped me. "What made you go to the middle one immediately?"

Without thinking about it, I simply spoke, "The colors and simplicity of it. It wasn't overwhelming, but the colors were friendly and brought your eyes immediately to the main frame of the picture."

She nodded. Her eyes met mine and crinkled around the edges with thought. "You know, I have never seen someone have such instincts when it comes to cover art. That is usually the toughest part to nail down." We moved from meeting to meeting until noon. Gayle was relentless in what she expected from her employees, but she was soft-spoken and obviously her employees enjoyed working with her.

She continued down the hall into an empty conference room. I followed her lead and sat down after she sat down. My notes in front of me, I wondered what was next for the day. My head pounded with all the information I had taken in and I was ready for a nap. If I landed this job, it would be exhausting to learn everything. Gayle had a quiet demeanor around the staff, yet she commanded attention as soon as she walked in the room. I had yet to see her demanding and unreasonable, but she controlled every meeting she had been in today.

The room was silent and Gayle made no effort to say anything. I mentally went through the past few hours and meetings I had attended. None of my excitement had waned during these meetings, if anything I was more pumped up to get this job. If only I could read Gayle and get an indication of what she was thinking.

"I noticed you took a lot of notes this morning. Any questions for me?" Gayle's soft voice broke through my thinking.

"Not really. I think there is a lot to take it, but the more I saw today, the more excited I am to learn the process better."

She nodded slowly. "I was impressed. You came prepared today to learn, not just observe, which so many automatically think that's what I mean when I say shadow me."

"The way I see it, this was an opportunity for me. I could either come and shadow you and just watch, or I could come and learn and even if this job doesn't work out for me, then I will have that much more knowledge to work with."

A slow smile spread across her face. "Excellent. I like that attitude."

The receptionist walked in with a folder in her hand and slid it Gayle. "Thank you, Penny." Gayle dismissed her. She then slid it to me. I made no move to open it, but waited.

"Go ahead and look at it." Gayle sat back. "It's a job offer."

I opened the folder and inspected the contents. The job description was on the left-hand side of the folder listing the job duties that had been in the advertisement for the job, as well as a second sheet that expanded all the duties and added more to it. It would be a demanding job and expected work hours were anywhere from fifty to sixty hours a week as needed.

The right-hand side of the folder contained a benefit package of insurance and paid time off as well as a salary offer. I swallowed when I saw the number. It was a number I never expected and certainly wasn't about to turn down. I closed the folder and looked up to meet Gayle's eyes.

"If you would like some time to think about it, maybe you would like to give me a call on Monday..."

I shook my head. "Thank you for that offer to think about it, but I'm prepared to answer you now. This is a job that I was instantly drawn to when I read the advertisement. After having the opportunity this morning to learn even more, there is no doubt this is the job for me. I accept your offer." I extended my right hand to her.

Gayle accepted my hand and smiled. "Welcome aboard. Let me show you where you will be and we'll talk starting date. I know you need to nail down an apartment and make moving arrangements. Will a month give you enough time to do that?"

"It should be ample time."

"Perfect. Use that letter of job offer with your salary to secure an apartment." We had been walking back to her office. She paused long enough for me to pick up my purse. "My office will be moving by the time you get moved here. I'll show you where we will end up."

We were walking once again farther down the hall. As we rounded the corner there was a desk in a small foyer off the main hallway with another office behind it. "This is where we will be. This will be your desk, and of course, my office through there. This will be a bit quieter farther away from reception."

"Thank you, Ms. Sutherland. I really appreciate you taking this chance on me."

"Please, if we are going to be working together and we will be working closely together, call me Gayle."

"Thank you, Gayle."

She smiled. "Again, welcome aboard. You have my contact number and email in the packet. Please email me specifics of your move once you know what is going on. I would like to start you out on reading some of the unsolicited manuscripts we get as soon as you can handle it, even if you aren't here yet. And no worries, once you start reading if you haven't moved yet, your pay will start."

I nodded, taking it all in. "I can start whenever you need me."

"Good. I'll have IT set up your email with the company and forward it to your personal email. Once you have access, we'll get you started."

Just like that I had a job and my life had turned around for the best already. I knew this was going to be a challenging month to get everything moved and settled in, but I was up for the challenge. Anything to move away from New Hampshire and the memories that haunted me there.

ten

The car was loaded. My parents were frustrated that I refused to let them come along. This was a journey I needed to make on my own as I traveled from the past to the future, or at least to the present, and rid myself of the past.

I had never again spoken of Jack to anyone. The hurt in his eyes still haunted my dreams. But the tears didn't come every night anymore and the pain had dulled to an ache instead of a sharp stabbing in my heart.

I gave Mom and Dad a hug as I closed the back hatch and headed to the driver's side. I heard the usual "be careful", "don't talk to strangers" warnings from my mother. I saw in her eyes fear of my leaving. Why? Because she couldn't control me anymore or was it more than that? It didn't matter. I made my decision and I was sticking to it. This was a new adventure for me, one that I had high hopes for.

With every mile that passed, my excitement grew. I had landed the perfect job. I was headed to a small studio apartment that overlooked the Chesapeake Bay. It had a small love seat and one of those beds that folded into the wall, along with a small kitchenette off to the side. The bathroom was barely big enough to stand in, but it would do until I could settle in. A year in a small place was do-able and I looked forward to the new start. I had bought some new dishes and a few pots and pans, but other than that my car was loaded simply with my clothes and my beloved records. Music had been a lifesaver for me as it helped me sort through my emotions.

I had not found closure with Jack. He was on my mind constantly. I heard recently from his sister that he had started dating and it was looking serious. The pain had hit me full force again at that news. My stomach clenched and the sharp stabbing pain in my heart was back. He had moved on quickly and in my mind just proved to me that I had made the right decision. There wasn't a day that didn't go by that I didn't think of him. I hoped he had found happiness and what he wanted in life. Yet, I ached for him still, an ache that couldn't be described but was as physical as it was emotional.

The anxiety of the move was overshadowed by my excitement to get in the car and crank up the tunes. Music that could soothe the pain of Jack's moving on. The healing elements of music I had clung to through this time. The miles flew by in time to the rhythm of the music. With the window down, I sang along to the radio, bee-bopping to the music in my seat. It was free-ing. I could feel the darkness lift from me as I drove on.

As evening approached, I entered Virginia. It had been a long day of driving but now I was close to being home. *Home.* A new home for me. It represented hope in my life.

I finally arrived in front of my new apartment at eight o'clock. I had arranged to meet the landlord at this time and found him standing in front of the building. He had just arrived. He helped me carry my meager belongings into the apartment. As I talked with him while signing the lease, I learned a bit about my neighbors. The building was a quiet group of professionals that worked hard and pretty much kept to themselves. There were a couple of tenants that were also pursuing a college degree and were seldom around.

After he left, I sank into the sofa and looked around. This was it. The living space was littered with boxes of clothes and my possession, but this was my home. It was quaint and was decorated in neutral tones. From the sofa, I could look out onto the balcony and out to the water. It would be peaceful to sit and listen to the water lapping the beach area. I looked around at the stacked boxes we had put against the wall, suitcases in the middle of the floor and sighed. I didn't have the energy to tackle taking care of things today. My refrigerator was bare so groceries were a top priority in the morning.

Tonight, I was ready to curl up in bed and sleep. The landlord had showed how to bring the bed down from the wall, and I made up the bed with fresh sheets I had bought. Double checking the locks on the door, I settled into bed and listened to the new sounds that surrounded me. There was no fear at this new adventure, and once again before exhaustion overtook, my last thoughts were of Jack.

• • •

Finally arriving in the office my first day was like old hat. Gayle and I had been in communication daily since I had taken the job. I had already read a dozen manuscripts and even recommended a couple of them to her. She was demanding, yet fair and certainly didn't want to overwhelm me.

I waved to Penny as I walked through reception and headed to my desk. Gayle had already told me that she was going to be late today so I could settle in and just get used to the calendar on the computer and the email system. I didn't expect a lot, but when I sat down and opened my email I was shocked to see over fifty unread emails. Most were from an artist in the cover art department as well as from Gayle herself with instructions for different projects that were going on that she wanted me to jump right in on.

Deep breath.

What had I gotten myself into? So much for a slow start on the first day.

I meticulously went through each email, making notes on questions I had regarding the projects, making a mental note to ask Gayle whether she wanted to discuss each of these or if I should just email her back with questions replying to the different emails on different projects. My mind was spinning by the time Gayle came around the corner.

"Good morning, Isabelle." Her chipper attitude immediately brought a smile to my face. "Thought you could use a mid-morning pick me up." She placed a steaming mug of coffee on my desk.

"Thank you, and good morning." I stood. I took a brief second to inhale the rich aroma of the coffee before taking a blissful sip. Oh, that hit the spot. I set my coffee down to head around the desk to go into her office when she came out with her own coffee in hand.

"Sit." She dragged the extra chair in the office up to my desk. "I'm sure you have questions so let's talk before we jump into anything else."

I sighed softly and took another sip of coffee. "Thank you for this. Yes, I was a bit overwhelmed when I saw my email box this morning."

Gayle laughed. "I figured you would be. Welcome to publishing."

I spent the next half hour with her answering all the questions I had regarding the projects. Instructions were given on what I could handle on my own and when I would be working with her on. By the time my coffee was done, I was too. Lord, I would never remember this. I took notes that I would be able to work from and felt semi-confident on how my week would go.

"Isabelle, I know this is a lot, but don't hesitate to ask questions. I don't expect you to get everything at once. I will be signing off on everything you do so don't worry about it having to be perfect. Perfection we strive for, but I know it's not immediate."

"Thank you."

The rest of the day flew by as I worked through projects. I made a task list that I could tackle in the morning. I already had another manuscript that needed to be read tonight when I got home, at least started. God, I hoped I could stay awake long enough to get going on it. My head was pounding.

Gayle had left an hour earlier to go to a dinner meeting. I looked up when I finished the last of the planning for the next day only to realize it was already seven p.m. I needed to grab some food, a glass of wine and curl up with this manuscript. I prayed it was good enough to hold my attention.

Knowing full well I was too tired to cook, and would be useless as soon as I walked through the door of my apartment, I stopped by a small Chinese place and picked up some vegetable Lo-Mein and beef teriyaki to go. Once inside my apartment, I immediately changed out of my dress and heels for the comfort of yoga pants and an over-sized t-shirt.

Grabbing a glass of wine and a fork from the kitchen, I curled up on the couch and opened the manuscript, eating as I read. I put the manuscript down only to go pour another glass of wine and put the left overs in the frig. The book had hooked me and this was definitely one I would be writing up as a recommendation for Gayle to look at.

eleven

Time flew by. Days turned into months and months into years. Before I knew it, I had engrossed myself into work as much as Gayle was and everyone in the office knew it. We had become quite the team. Acquisitions were at an all-time high on Gayle's team as I had found some new authors that were worth pursuing. Gayle was grooming me to become a junior editor. She would hire another assistant and I would be able to acquire new authors and work directly with them, with Gayle still signing off on all projects. I thrived in this environment. Most days while at work, or even at home if I was still working, I kept my focus off Jack and the incredible sense of guilt and loneliness I still felt after all these years.

The rare moments I allowed myself the luxury of sitting and thinking were painful reminders of my failures in life. Yes, I was successful in my job, but my personal life was an utter failure. I was alone and married to my work.

In some respects, it was just what I needed and others, I longed for someone to come home to at night, to share my dreams and fears with. Someone like Jack...he had listened to me when I chose to tell him things, and I had listened to his dreams for the future.

I wondered if he had accomplished all he had hoped for. I knew by this time he was married with children and yet, I couldn't help but wonder if he was happy, or at least content. Life was a strange journey to travel. There could be moments of pure happiness and joy, and then loneliness could hit you whether you were sitting there alone or if you were surrounded by a million people. Depression still plagued me, but I kept a stoic face and no one was wiser for the battles that raged inside of me.

I loved my job, but life continued to cut me down at the knees in my personal life on a daily basis. Some days it was a struggle to even get out of bed and focus on what had to be done, but day by day I proved to myself what a master of disguises I was and how little anyone really knew me.

Tonight was no different. I had actually finished the newest manuscript I'd been reading earlier. With my glass of wine, I had ventured to the balcony of my apartment to listen to the ocean. This was the one constant in my life that I craved daily. I needed to hear the waves and smell that salt air. It kept me sane.

The salt air tonight was bringing me back to Portsmouth, New Hampshire. The days that I had spent walking the mall replaying that last night when I had pushed Jack so far, he had walked away for good. The sadness and hurt in his blues eyes still haunted me. The wetness on my cheeks brought to the realization that I was once again crying at the memories that flooded me.

Jack Riley.

The one that had gotten away. There was no doubt in my mind that love still lingered in my heart for him. The stabbing hurt in my heart wouldn't be so great if it didn't. Even the guilt had lessened a bit over the years, but the shattering of my heart-- my own doing--had never healed. I had no desire to let another man in. As far as I was concerned I had made my choice and in pushing Jack away, I had sabotaged my own future. The loneliness was nothing more than what I deserved after the horrid treatment I had put Jack through. He had to hate me. I couldn't imagine that he could ever forgive me for not trusting him.

Fear to even try again held me paralyzed. My answer was always *no* to the friends that wanted to set me up, or to the men that had asked me out. I couldn't go through that again, or put someone else through it. And if there was one thing I had learned about myself is that I was destined to be alone. Self-sabotaging had become second nature to me and thankfully it did not carry over into my work as it was the one area of my life that held success.

Glass raised high, I saluted Jack and the memory of the man I had given my heart to along with the only gift I had to give. The man that held everything of me and didn't even know he had it. What a coward I had been. I had allowed Jack's choice of the word *obligation* to scare the hell out of me and allowed my mother to play right into that with I had no right to be happy since the suicide attempt.

What no one realized was there wasn't a day that didn't go by that I didn't think about the attempt or what would have been had I succeeded. I was thankful for my job that I loved, but I could have done without my personal life being nothing but an empty shell of what ifs.

I needed more. But did I dare open my heart and try again? Could I find the courage to even just find a male friend – one who could be nothing more than just that? I wanted so badly to break through the loneliness and sadness that gripped me at times, but I couldn't shake the anxiety of the chance of failure again. The thought of giving my heart to someone else who might not realize it and then walk away like Jack did was devastating. The guilt hit me just like it did every time. This was not Jack's fault. I had done this to myself. I broke my own heart and had no idea how to pick up the pieces again.

Downing the last of my wine, I shook off the nostalgia and closed my eyes. I focused on the sounds of the waves and allowed them to comfort me. Each wave that hit the beach, washed over me and took a little bit more of my stress away. My mantra with each wave ran through my mind – *I can do this. I can do this.* The last of the tension lifted off my shoulders and I inhaled deeply, held it for a moment before exhaling slowly. The last of the expelled breath left my body and took with it the stress of the memories I had allowed myself to feel.

It was going to be another long day at work tomorrow and I needed sleep, but first I had a report sheet to fill out on the latest manuscript. It was one that I wanted to take on and I knew that Gayle would need a bit more convincing than usual for this author. The writing was rough, but my gut was telling me this was a very talented writer than just needed some guidance.

twelve

Time passed way too quickly. Days turned into months and months turned into years. I had worked hard at my job and received promotions and raises through the years. I had traded in the small studio apartment for a one bedroom down the street from my starting point where I could still overlook the Bay. I couldn't fathom the thought of moving somewhere away from the water. The sounds of the waves had become my music at night. I would sit on the balcony and watch it as the moon shined down and caused it to shimmer.

Jack was still present in my thoughts and I wondered often how he was and if he was happy. The hurt of his eyes that last day haunt me still. Every December 28 I found myself mourning the love I had found. There are tears and huge amounts of alcohol that help numb the pain. I move through December preceding the 28 with dread, knowing where my mind will go and having no power to control the memories that will flood me that day. But each year I welcomed the pain, a pain deserving for someone who had cruelly hurt the one thing in my life that had been great. I had done this to myself and changed my path forever.

Ironically it was no longer the suicide attempt that defined me, but my choice to push Jack away. That one foolish decision had been such a pivotal movement that changed my life path forever. That decision would haunt me forever and would become the greatest regret of my life. Even years later it felt like those five weeks never existed. There had never been a mention of Jack from anyone.

As I sat on my balcony, celebrating my twenty-fifth birthday alone, I raised my glass of wine in a silent toast to those moments that I tried to run from and realized that they are still with me. The tears coursed silently down my face before I even realized I was crying. It was just another birthday. No reason for tears, and yet, it was not the age that was getting to me or even the fact that I sat here alone. It was the lack of hope I had for ever having someone in my life that brought me as much joy as Jack did. It was impervious to think that this was my life, and yet I couldn't bring myself to wish for more.

Seven years had passed since I walked away, or more accurately forced Jack to walk away, from what we had and I still couldn't forget him. The emotions were still just as strong and so much a part of my life day to day. I close my eyes and allow the memories to creep in. I see him lying next to me in his barracks, my head on his chest and allow myself to feel the warmth of him. The memories are so visceral to me still. I feel the heat of his body warm mine next to him, I can feel his fingers tracing up and down on my back and it still brings a heat and ache to me. How I wished we had shared more than just one day of sex...I still wanted more of him and had no right to think that way.

He moved on and married, even had kids, according to what his sister had told my parents. My hand subconsciously moved to my abdomen. There were still times I wished I had gotten pregnant with his child. To have something of him, something that was a part of both of us to hold on to. Instead I had nothing of Jack's except an old picture that was taken on Christmas Eve. It sat framed on my bureau where I could see it every day. That probably wasn't healthy, but I couldn't force myself to pack the picture away. The two of us, smiling, his arm around me. There was a connection and I threw it all away.

I could spend the time beating myself up and I knew I needed to move on. I took a deep breath and push my Jack out of my mind. I couldn't help but refer to him as my Jack.

Okay, girl, get it together.

I downed the remainder of my wine and pour another glass. The bottle sat empty beside me. Well, one thing I have learned, no matter how much I drink, I couldn't get rid of the past and its memories that haunted me. In fact, sometimes the memories were strongest when the wine bottle was empty.

This was it. My first quarter of a century behind me. Reflection took over as I had been journaling a lot lately. I pulled out the notebook and started my annual birthday reflection. The page was already set with the WHAT HAVE I ACCOMPLISHED column and the WHAT'S NEXT column.

Accomplishments. Hmmmm, I had to think hard. It had been a good past year. I had been promoted at work. I loved the job, although it was demanding. Gayle and I had established a good rapport and she had groomed me well for the position. I was her right hand, and yet had freedom to bring in new authors I felt were worthy.

Okay, good job in column one. I had also started saving more regularly. Yup, that was an accomplishment for a girl who loved to shop. I had cut back on the number of shoes I thought I needed and put the money into savings instead.

Okay, it may not seem like a huge accomplishment, but at this junction in my life I counted everything. Small steps. I had learned over the past seven years to count my blessings. Moving to the GOALS column, I started the list.

New car

Go back to college

Get out more

It wasn't a lot, but it was a start and good enough for the annual list. Over the years, my lists hadn't increase much, but there usually was only one or two accomplishments and two or three goals. Each year I would add go back to college, and it was yet to make it to the accomplishment side of the annual list.

One of these days…that was what I kept telling myself. One of these days I would do everything I always wanted to. I also wanted to travel, but that wasn't going on the goal list because it was a far-fetched dream. I spent hours surfing the internet about different places to travel and travel packages that were available. But it always came down to never wanting to go alone somewhere. It was hard enough getting out of the house beyond work. Although occasionally I will go out with some of my coworkers for a drink or two.

As the last of the wine in my glass was gulped down, I gazed down to the water. The moon beam across the water shimmered. The little sparkles like small diamonds stretched across the beam of light for as far as the eye could see.

thirteen

The sun blinded me as it splayed across my bed. The bottle of wine from the night before that I had consumed threatened to tear my head wide open. When would I learn to not drink the full bottle by myself? I dragged myself from the bed and made my way to the bathroom. A hot shower eased the ache in my head somewhat. Once the coffee started brewing, I stood at my sliding door to the balcony and looked over the water.

The beeping of the coffeemaker, signaling the brew cycle was done, grabbed my attention. Pouring a mug with just a bit of creamer in it, I took my usual first sniff of the coffee, inhaling the rich aroma deeply before taking a sip. It never failed to perk me up. I closed the lid on my travel mug and headed for the door. The best place to get rid of a headache, in my opinion, was a walk along the water.

Armed with my coffee and flip flops ready to be kicked off as soon as I hit the beach, I headed out. I hadn't even gotten as far as the bottom of the stairs before my cell phone beeped. I glanced at it briefly and seeing a text from one of my co-workers, I slipped it into my back pocket. Heidi was great, but she always wanted to up the ante so to speak on birthdays and I just wasn't in the mood for what kind of off the wall adventure she had come up with at the moment.

Hitting the beach, I slipped off the flip-flops and walked the distance of the beach to the rock cluster at the end of the sandy beach. I had a favorite rock to sit at. The way it connected with another rock, made the perfect chair, back and all, for me to sit against and hear the water hitting the rocks. There was nothing like that sound to wash away the stress from my shoulders. As I settled against the rock, sipping my coffee, I closed my eyes and allowed the gentle sea breeze to soothe away the headache. The water crashing against the rocks lulled me into a sense of peace, allowing me to relax and enjoy the moment. This right here was my heaven.

I could die and have my ashes scattered right here and I would be happy.

I heard the muttering "Shit" sounding like it was right next to me and my eyes flew open. Standing not far from me was a man about my age, looking down at his coffee, spilled on the rock below him.

"Oh, that's not good." I felt for the guy. I would be miserable without my coffee.

"Yeah, you startled me. I didn't expect someone in my spot on a Sunday morning." His snarky attitude immediately set me on edge.

"Your spot? I'm here all the time." I stretched out my legs, took a sip of my coffee before I saluted him with it.

"Nice. Rub it in that you have your coffee in hand

and mine is being enjoyed by the barnacles." A slight twinge of humor came through and I snickered. I wasn't in the sharing mood, but the man did just lose his coffee.

"Have a seat." I slid over just a hair on the rock. It was definitely big enough for two, albeit cozy.

He sighed as he slid onto the rock next to me. He tried not to sit too close, yet our thighs touched and I didn't want to appear that I was disgusted and pull away, so I left my leg there. Midsummer and he obviously was a man that liked to be in the sun. He was quite tan, and he showed it off with shorts and a tank top. His biceps were muscular, but not bulging. If I had to guess, I would assume from the muscle tone in his legs he was a runner and possibly did some small weight lifting for upper body strength.

"I'm Nick Sterling." He finally spoke.

"Isabelle." I sipped my coffee again and then felt self-conscious with it as his sat in shock contrast to the dry rocks around to the coffee laden one.

"Thankfully it was my second cup today so I'm not a complete crank to be around," he said with a sideways glance.

I tried not to smile, but the corners of my mouth betrayed me. I quickly lifted my coffee mug to try and hide it.

"You can't hide it. Go ahead and laugh at me." He mocked.

"Look, I didn't drop your coffee. This is my first cup and I'm not even halfway through it yet, so I may not be totally coherent."

Nick grinned. "Oh, so you're not just really quiet, you're saving me from the brutal attack of your coffee-deprived mindless chatter."

"Coffee-deprived mindless chatter? Good lord, you

really needed that second cup to speak intelligently." I bantered back.

I leaned against the rock again and closed my eyes. The headache was better, but was still a nagging ache. I just wanted quiet. I felt Nick's leg press against mine as he shifted his position. He moved again and his leg moved away from mine. I finally opened one eye and looked at him.

"You about done moving?"

He chuckled. "No, you are hogging the best part of the rock." He nudged me with his elbow.

I sighed. "Fine. Have your precious rock." I stood as to leave and he reached for my hand, grasping it with his. Heat shot up my arm as I looked down at him.

"I was kidding. Please stay."

I shook my head. "I would love to, but I thought the air would help my headache and it hasn't. I think I'll go get some more coffee."

"Not enough sleep or overindulgence last night?"

"Birthday celebration." I refused to clarify that I had definitely overindulged or the fact that I had done it alone.

"Happy birthday."

"Did I say it was my birthday?" I was feeling snarky and just wanted to get away.

"Um, no, I guess not. I just assumed." Nick released my hand.

"Well, thanks." I turned to pick my way among the rocks to the sandy beach again.

"Thanks? Ah-ha, it was your birthday." Nick followed me and I turned when I got to the sandy beach.

"Are you following me?" The tone must have been a bit harsher than I expected as he took a step back and almost tripped over a rock.

"No. I thought when you said get more coffee that I really could use a second cup too."

"That wasn't an offer." Irritation laced my words.

"Didn't think so. I live up the beach a way, thought I'd go home *alone* and get another cup."

I felt like a fool for assuming the worst in him. "I'm sorry. Not at my best this morning. It was nice to meet you, Nick."

He smiled. "I'd say the same, but I'm afraid for what you might read into it." He waved as he started jogging up the beach.

My eyes stayed on him as I watched him run along the edge of the water. Slowly I started walking after him, or at least along the beach in the same direction. He was a good view to follow and I smiled to myself. I could still appreciate a good-looking guy when I saw one and oh, my what a nice backside he had. I was grinning when I arrived at my apartment and the headache had gone. The second cup of coffee was still necessary to wake me up and get me focused for the day.

I took that second cup out to the balcony and allowed the sun's warmth to wash over me. Sunglasses in place and my coffee in hand, I was once again relaxed and happy. For all the times I had sat at the rock chair, I had never met Nick. What did he mean his spot? Of course I did tend to go more in the evenings than in the mornings so maybe he was the morning guy who took up resident there. Maybe I would just need to change my time of day to enjoy that spot and hopefully run into him again.

I perked up as I saw him walk back along the beach. He couldn't have gone too far, as he was walking with a travel mug in his hand so he obviously had gotten his coffee. I sat forward in my chair to watch him. He appeared to be scanning the apartments along the way instead of looking at the water. I sat back and wondered if he could see me.

He stopped and looked closely at my building, but I couldn't tell if he could make out anyone on the balcony or not. I sat as still as I could, praying I blended in with the balcony and pretty remained unseen. He sipped his coffee as he kept his eyes on the building. Okay, it was just getting creepy now. I stood and went inside. As I shut the door, I glanced and he was still standing there before turning to view the water. I shut my shades and watched from the corner and he just didn't move. Okay, what was he pulling?

It seemed like an eternity that I watched him, although it probably was less than five minutes before he sauntered down the beach towards the rocks again. The way he moved led me to believe that he thought I was watching him, although he couldn't know that. I was behind closed shades.

I was intrigued and wanted to know more, but couldn't allow myself that luxury. Falling for one man had already been enough for me, even if it had been seven years prior. I had never truly given my heart a chance to fall for someone else. Jack was still so much about of my life in the way that held onto my heart. I had had no contact with him since that fateful day in the mall, the day the hurt in his eyes shattered my heart. It wasn't his fault. I had done it to myself by not trusting him enough to tell him of my past. I had forced the only good thing in my life to walk away from me. Would I ever get over it? Ever get over Jack?

My heart still ached when I thought of him. The sharp stabbing pain was no longer, but the ache was enough to

bring me to tears still. Seven years later. But, feeling curious about Nick, well that was a good thing, right?

My mind wandered to the beach that morning. He
was a good-looking guy, with a sarcastic sense of humor.
I loved that. Sarcasm was a language, and so few understood it in me. There was only one thing to do. Put the
past truly behind me and move forward. I often wondered
where Jack was and how his life had turned out. Did he
ever think of her? If only I could get through one day
where he didn't drift into my mind.

Life had been difficult at times for me. The move had
definitely been a good one for me, one where I was able to
distance myself from the negativity I had once felt in my
life. But the past had also shaped me into the person I was
– a loner. One that stayed away from relationships of any
kind whether it be romantic or friendships. The only way to
protect myself was to shield myself from anything or anyone
that could allow me to become vulnerable and open.

Closing yourself off from people though could be a
lonely thing. I allowed myself a few fun moments with
co-workers, but even they didn't know much about me.
I had built a solid wall around my heart. I longed for the
days when I had been hopeful about love and believed
that love could actually conquer all hard times. Would
Jack have been that rock I longed for in my life? Could I
still find that if I allowed myself a certain amount of vulnerability? Could I control how vulnerable I became and
still allow someone else in?

Shutting off my thoughts of Jack, I was determined
to get out more and see if I could reacquaint myself with
the world and dating. I needed to move forward and find
someone, whether a man to be in a relationship with or
just a lover that could give me the sexual release I needed

and then allow me to hide myself away from any emotions. Maybe that was how I needed to jump back into it – just find a lover and ignore all the other aspects of it. After all, sexual release could cure a lot of heartache and loneliness.

I was determined to make something of my life and I didn't need a man to get in the way of that. A man would insist that I set my dreams and goals aside to support theirs. I had built up the wall so high around my heart that I couldn't even see around it sometimes to see what might be good in my life and what I should be protecting myself from.

The house was becoming claustrophobic and I hadn't seen if Nick had walked by. I needed to smell the salt water and hear the waves. It was my stress reliever and helped me forget the past that all too often seeped in my thoughts as hard as I tried to keep them out. I grabbed a bottle water and headed back across the street. I would stay away from the rocks. Grabbing my beach chair next to the door, just sitting with my feet in the water would help.

I parked myself just where my feet would be in a couple of inches of the water as the waves came in and out. I closed my eyes and leaned back in my chair, listening to the water, allowing the sound of it to wash over me. I had almost been lulled into a meditation when I felt someone next to me. A shadow fell across me and I opened my eyes to look up into those blue eyes looking down at me.

"Afraid to come back to the rocks?" Nick snickered.

"Didn't want to upset you."

"You didn't upset me…surprised me is more accurate."

"What are you doing here?" I raised my hand to keep the sun out of my eyes while I was looking up at him.

"Walking back to my house." He raised his travel

mug. "I had kind of hoped you would grab another cup of coffee and come back to the rock."

"Why would you hope that?" I was at a loss as to what I should be saying to this man while he looked down at me.

"I enjoyed meeting you."

I feigned shock. "You could've fooled me."

"Can I make it up to you for the way I acted this morning?" Sincerity was written all over his face.

"There's no need." I rose from my chair. I needed a more even footing when talking to this man. He was throwing me off balance.

He searched my face, but his own face was unreadable. "Broken heart, not into men?"

I laughed out loud and watched his face break into a grin. "Neither, thanks."

"Okay, so you *do* like men then I might still have a chance."

I shook my head. "You are impossible, you realize that?"

Nick shrugged. "Is that a bad thing? Most females complain if I guy gives up too soon."

"Is this a ploy to make me feel bad for you? Obviously your experience is being rejected by women and you give up." I reached for my chair to fold it up.

"Running away from me again?"

"No, I was thinking I might actually need to get something done today instead of just sitting on the beach."

"Isabelle, I really would like to get to know you a bit. Can we meet for dinner? Coffee? Drinks?" Nick watched me.

"I don't know…" My mind was screaming no, but I thought to my resolution to move forward. What would it hurt? "Okay."

Nick grinned. "Okay, then. How about dinner later

tonight?" He pointed to a small seafood place at the edge of the pier down the beach.

"At that dive?" It was my favorite place in the world.

"Dive?" Nick clenched his hand over his heart. "You cut me to the quick, woman. It's my favorite place."

"A drama queen, I see. I love the food there."

"Great, I'll see you at six tonight."

He didn't wait for an answer, but gave me a small salute and started down the beach. What had I just gotten myself into? And yet as I headed back to my apartment, my heart was racing with anticipation almost as fast as my mind raced with what I could wear.

Fourteen

The rest of the day sped by as I dug out every piece of clothing I owned in my closet. The bed was covered with outfits that I had tried on and discarded. It shouldn't be this hard to meet a guy for dinner. It was dinner, nothing more. I finally, for the third time, tried on a new sundress I had bought the week before. It was a jade green in color and made my eyes look even greener. This was the one. I felt good it in, sexy. It had been a long time since I felt I wanted to look sexy for someone.

Sexy. What an odd concept. I had no idea how to look sexy, but this dress made me feel sexy although I looked the same. What was it about the way the world's conception of what was sexy made us panic over a date? I took a deep breath.

Not. Going. To. Panic.

It was dinner. My favorite food so I wouldn't have to worry about what to order and the owners were friends of mine. Oh, no, what if they were friends of Nick's too? I had rejected their efforts to introduce me to their single friend that was nearby. Oh, God, please don't let it be Nick. If things didn't work out, I would never be able to show my face there again.

I glanced at my watch. It was ten minutes to six and it would take me about that long to walk down to the restaurant. I slipped my feet into a pair of white sandals that strapped crisscrossed and strapped up above my ankles, but thankfully they were flats so walking the distance wouldn't be an issue. I used to wear heels all the time, but now living near the beach, I was barefoot constantly and couldn't wear the heels more than five minutes without my feet killing me.

As I got closer I could see Nick standing outside. His blue jeans fit nicely as well as the sky-blue polo he had on. It clung to his muscles, but not too tight that one would think he was arrogant. The butterflies in my stomach started fluttering and I inhaled deeply, exhaling slowly.

"You look beautiful." The words were a rush as Nick watched me approach.

"Thank you. You don't look so bad yourself."

He opened the door and I went in before him. A gentleman, too. So far first impressions were good, on my end anyway. Other than the obvious approval at what I was wearing, Nick was unreadable. I tried to not let that freak me out, but I wanted some sort of sign that he was actually enjoying himself. He was quiet as we sat in a corner booth and looked at the menus. I already knew what I wanted, but used the moment to watch him from behind the menu. He seemed totally engrossed in the menu.

I set my menu aside and openly watched him. I was

strangely curious as to this man who seemed sarcastic and snarky, but tonight seemed quiet.

"Already know what you want?" Nick glanced up.

"Yup. Always get the same thing."

Nick moved his menu aside. "Me too, but I keep thinking I'm going to change it to something different."

"Don't let me stop you. Peruse away and see if something else strikes your fancy."

Nick grinned. "I have what strikes my fancy right in front of me."

The meaning was perfectly clear and I felt my face flush.

"Is it possible that you are even more beautiful when you blush?" Nick murmured.

I had no words to respond, but felt the blush deepen. I was thankful at that moment for the waitress to show up and take our order.

"Izzy, the usual?"

I nodded, embarrassed that I was known by name.

"How about you, Nick, same thing for you too?" I glanced up at Kelli. She knew him by name too. Kelli winked at me as Nick nodded also and handed her the menus.

"It's about time I saw you two in here together."

I groaned inwardly. Crap, this was my worst nightmare and judging from Nick's face, it was his also.

Nick spoke as soon as Kelli moved away from the table. "I'm sorry. I didn't give it a thought that Kelli would give us a hard time."

"How long have you known her?"

"Since I moved to the area. It was one of the first places I ate at, regularly apparently, as she struck up a conversation with me on about the third visit interrogating me where I lived, if I was single. I should have known better than to bring you here."

I had been trying to hide my laughter. I knew all too well Kelli's interrogation style as I had been the brunt of it for too many years. "I get it. Been there and done that. I was afraid she would say something."

The awkwardness had been broken thanks to Kelli and I was able to relax. Those blue eyes kept my eyes focused on his while he talked. We talked about what brought us to Virginia and how long we had been there. We skirted around relationship talk, past or present, for which I was grateful.

Time passed quickly as we ate and talked. Laughter was quick to flow with the sarcastic humor I found Nick had that matched mine. For the first time in a long time I was content with the night. As the table was cleared around us, the feeling of claustrophobia came over me.

"How about a walk along the water?" Nick seemed to read my mind.

I nodded and stood. We were silent as we made our way to the beach. I undid the straps on my sandals and slid them off my feet. Unaware of Nick watching me, I sighed as I felt the sand between my toes. Nick reached for my hand and without word, laced his fingers through mine as we started walking down the beach. There was no need for words, as we strolled hand in hand. My thoughts for once slowed and I let the softness of the small waves lapping the beach soothe my nerves.

I started to slow as we neared my apartment, but Nick squeezed my hand. I kept walking knowing we were headed back to the rocks. He continued to hold my hand as I maneuvered the rocks barefoot to get to the sitting spot. I sat down and Nick sat close, his thigh pressed against mine, with my hand still clasped tightly in his. I watched the water and the gentle waves coming in and out as the moon shined upon it. It always took my breath away, the majestic beauty of it. It was so much bigger than I was, making my life seem insignificant, and yet important at the same time.

"I really enjoyed spending time with you tonight, Isabelle." Nick's voice was quiet and I could feel his eyes upon me.

"I enjoyed it too." I turned to face him and found him closer than I expected. I knew by the look in his eyes that the kiss was inevitable. We both wanted it and I was powerless to stop it if I had wanted to.

"Izzy, huh?" He smiled, his face still just inches from mine.

"Called by a few close friends." I wanted to see those eyes, but it was just dark enough the blueness was hidden.

"Izzy it is." The words were barely loud enough to hear, but as they registered with my brain, Nick moved forward and captured my lips with his. The kiss deepened and I sighed as I leaned into him. My free hand slid up around his neck and pulled him closer. By the time we broke from the kiss, we both were breathless.

I leaned my forehead against his, trying to slow my breathing. My hand was still at the base of his neck and my fingers moved slowly against his skin. "Izzy, keep that up and this rock is going to become very uncomfortable."

I grinned, but moved my hand from his neck. Forehead to forehead, we sat there gazing into each other's eyes. I wanted more. I wanted to feel those lips on mine again, all over my body. I wanted to run my hands over him and tear that shirt off him and feel his toned abs beneath my fingers. I trembled as I tried to pull back and he held me close.

"Cold?"

I shook my head no, not trusting my voice. I leaned my head on his shoulder. I felt the tug to open my heart and the immediate panic starting to rise in me. There was always the push and pull to be open to someone, and risk the hurt. In reality, the hurt was by my own hand and I usually ended up hurting others more than I hurt myself.

"Izzy?" Nick's deep voice soothed the panic in me.

"Yes?"

He pulled his face back from mine without losing the closeness in which he held me. "You okay?"

I nodded. "It's probably time to call it a night, though. Early day tomorrow for me." No early day, but he didn't have to know that.

He stood and pulled me up with him, his fingers still laced with mine. He walked before me over the rocks, making sure I traversed them as nimbly has I had going up to the rock seat. Reaching the sand, we walked in silence back to beach area across from my apartment.

"This is where I say good night. Thank you for this evening. I thoroughly enjoyed it." I prayed he would just let me go and not insist on walking me to the building.

He pulled me close for another kiss, soft and gentle, teasing my tongue with his before breaking it off. "Good night, Izzy." He let go of my hand and took a step back.

I moved before I changed my mind and scurried to the building, upstairs to where I stood in the dark watching Nick, standing there on the beach just watching, waiting for my light to come on I assumed. After a few minutes, I flipped on the light and he turned to start down the beach towards his own home.

I poured myself a glass of wine and made my way to the balcony. Settling into my favorite chaise lounge, I sipped my wine and thought of the evening. Nick was a great guy, obviously attractive and there definitely was chemistry between us. So why the panic? Logically I needed to move forward and allow myself the opportunity for love to find me, but it wasn't a path I was eager to transverse. And logic was never my strong suit. I had worked so hard the past seven years to build walls, walls that kept that mushy sentimental stuff out and just because a man came along that could make my knees weak with one kiss, didn't mean I had to throw away all that protection for my heart.

We were adults. There is no reason we couldn't have a physical relationship without all that other *stuff* that got in the way of a good connection. I sighed. It was impossible for me to get past the hope that I could ever fall in love again. The last time had just about killed me, well, not literally, but the thought of that kind of pain – physical pain – I would never be able to handle again.

My mind wandered to Jack once again. Not a day went by that he didn't enter my thoughts. I no longer was thinking of him physically, sexually, but I always wondered where he was, how his life was going. Did he hate me for the way I handled things? He had to. There was no way a man could ever forget a woman for having sex with him and then pushing him away like he had done something wrong. It was unfathomable to me that he would even remember me beyond that one day we had in his barracks and I forced him to walk away from.

I had made sure he wouldn't have any warm, fuzzy thoughts about me and the day we spent together. Yet, that day still stood out as the best day of my life. The moment I realized what love was…and how I did long for that feeling again. The feeling to be loved and to be held.

fifteen

I had tossed and turned all night. Sleep had eluded and as I dragged myself from bed, towards the coffee maker that thankfully I had intuitively known to set up and put on timer. The rich aroma hit me as soon as I entered the kitchen. I inhaled deeply, allowing the full aroma to penetrate my sleep-deprived brain.

I poured my first mug and closed my eyes as I inhaled the scent. My morning ritual, inhaling the aroma before taking that first sip, that allowed me to fully taste the richness. I sighed as the first sip ran across my tongue and down my throat. The warmth spread through me as I made my way to the balcony.

The coffee and the sounds of the waves from the ocean worked their magic on me. The nagging lack of sleep headache faded and I found a renewed energy. I pulled myself together and poured a second cup of coffee in a travel mug. The rocks were where I needed to be to think – more likely overthink – what happened last night with Nick. The truth of the matter was I enjoyed his company, and was very physically attracted to him. A relationship was not what I wanted, but many were open to the idea of a sex-only relationship.

Headed to the rocks, yet taking my time along the water's edge, I allowed my mind to roam freely over the last night's events. Nick was charming and good company. And those blue eyes. A sigh escaped from me at the realization that once again I had found another man with my kryptonite – blue eyes. They kept me mesmerized and reeled me into more than I wanted, which was never a good thing for me.

Did I have the courage, or the will power, to walk away from what could be just another bad decision?

I settled into the rock seat and closed my eyes. The waves pounding against the rocks soothed my frazzled nerves. The warmth from the sun heated my skin as my mind was filled of the very scene that happened right here last night. Did it have to be a bad decision? Would I ever find a love that would heal my self-destructing pattern of life?

Life had become more complicated than it should be. I had spent the past seven years running from a broken heart that I had been responsible for breaking. I had thrown myself into empty relationship after empty relationship, enjoying the sex, but never allowing myself to enjoy the intimacy of the relationship. I would walk away at the first sign that any emotion was coming into play. I had become a master at shutting my emotions off and hardening my heart. It had become an extremely lonely life, and yet my thoughts were always on Jack.

The connection between us in such a short time had overwhelmed me and my young mind had no way of comprehending how to handle it. I had carried the burden of guilt over the way I had treated Jack and the hurt in his eyes as he walked away that last day haunted my days and my nights.

"Thought I might find you here." Nick's voice startled me into the present.

"Did you?" I squinted one eye open at him and took a sip of my coffee.

"Hoping maybe is the right word." He sat down on the rock next to me, yet made no move to touch me.

I could feel his presence next to me and it gave me a sense of security and yet threw me off balance at the same time. I shifted my position, keeping my eyes closed, hoping I could appear unaffected by him.

"How'd you sleep last night?" His voice was soft and deep, bringing out in me a longing to just lean against him.

I shrugged my shoulders.

His chuckle got my attention and I turned to look at him. "That good, huh?"

"Not well. You?"

"Not as well as I had hoped for, but I think we both know why." He reached his hand for mine and intertwined our fingers. I looked down at the hands and glanced back up at him. His blue eyes sparkled, reminding of the sky where the ocean met it.

"Really? Why is that?" I tried to keep my voice lighthearted.

"I know I was feeling a bit too lonely in my bed last night." Nick leaned towards me as if to kiss me, but stopped just shy. His lips curled into a half smile and he waited as I waited. Neither of us wanting to go that extra distance. For me the fear was palpable. Do I give into this – whatever this was? "Was your bed lonely too?"

My eyes moved to his lips as he practically whispered those words. I swallowed hard and nodded. "Nick…"

"Don't do it." He shook his head. "Don't overthink it."

"I can't." I moved back away from that kiss that was just hanging in the air between us, just waiting to happen.

"Can't? Or scared to?" He sat back and closed his eyes, his hand still hanging onto mine.

I had no answer for that. I sighed and just sat there in silence. The sounds of the waves resonated with me… why, why, why they seemed to say over and over again. I was a fool and I knew it, but yet I couldn't help myself from sabotaging everything that came my way.

I don't know how long we sat there in silence. In fact I'm pretty sure I started to drift off in the warmth of the sun, until I felt Nick shift. His thigh pressed against mine and his hand left mine. I started to open my eyes, just as he pulled me forward just enough to put his arm around me and pull me close to him. My head resting on his shoulder, I pushed away the immediate thoughts of why I shouldn't get this close and snuggled closer. I wanted his warmth, the false sense of safety I felt with his arm around me.

"Get some sleep. We're good right here unless the rock is too hard for you." I could feel the rumble in his chest as he spoke.

The rock, hard. It was almost laughable since I was leaning against his rock-hard chest. I would prefer to feel his rock hardness against me in a soft bed, but I wasn't ready to tell him that.

I don't know how long we sat there, but I do know the moment I allowed myself to finally relax. My body melted against his. His arm around me pulled me closer, if that was possible, his fingers lightly running up and down my arm. The soft sigh escaped me as I felt the strain of trying to hold myself at bay. I drifted into a light sleep, the rising and falling of his chest with every breath pulling me closer to total relaxation.

Lying against him with my head on his chest, I fought the wave of panic that washed over me at the realization of how relaxed I was. The panic pushed at me like the waves against the rocks, hitting me again and again until I couldn't fight it any longer. I sat up and pushed away from him, staring out into the ocean.

"Well, you relaxed all of thirty seconds maybe." Nick chuckled behind me. He had allowed me the space and made no move to touch me again. A part of me was relieved, while another part of me felt the immediate loss of his warmth. I shook my head. I couldn't have it both ways and I had no idea how far I would allow myself to open to him.

"Cute." I stood. "I've got to go. Things to do before I dive into the work week tomorrow."

• • •

I felt Nick's eyes on me as I walked as fast as I could without breaking into a jog. I needed to breathe. Nick made that impossible. Here was a man that I could relax around, but that was dangerous in itself. What if I relaxed and unintentionally opened my heart up? Nick had the power to hurt me and I couldn't allow that to happen. Nothing good ever came from someone giving their heart to another – at least not in my life.

I took the stairs two at a time to reach my apartment

and only released the breath I had apparently been holding once the door was shut and locked behind me. Melding into my true self, or the one I had perfected over the years, I switched to my professional persona and jumped back into the work I had left Friday night for a date with Nick. Engrossing myself in the newest read that had come through to me, I lost myself into the world of high speed chases and murder in this thriller.

It was just what I needed to take my mind off romance and the hot man who had just held me to his side so I could rest.

Coffee.

More coffee was needed if I was going to focus solely on the book and get my mind of Nick, who somehow kept creeping in my thoughts no matter what I was doing. There had been only one other man that had done that to me…Jack Riley.

Sighing in frustration, I gathered up my manuscript to head to the kitchen to make coffee. It was going to be a long day, but I wanted to finish this book before work tomorrow. Monday morning meetings were the day to pitch new books we wanted to take on. Gayle would expect a full report on anything I wanted to acquire.

The coffeemaker beeped, signaling the coffee was ready. I poured myself a mug and headed to the balcony. The area was shady now that the sun had moved enough and it was warm without the heat from the bright sun. The waves in the background helped me find my center and closing my eyes I took in the sound to find that grounding I needed to. Sipping my coffee, I opened my eyes and started reading.

I was transformed from the beach to the fast-paced life of New York City where a young girl ran for her life after witnessing a murder. Who would find her first? The killer or the detective who sworn he would save her? I was mesmerized by the story line and read it without paying much attention to the issues. I knew I would need to read this again to determine the areas that needed fixing, but in my mind if a book could keep my mind focused on the story and not the issues, then this was indeed a talented writer and deserved a chance to be published.

I sighed in contentment as I finished reading the last page. This was a great book and one I was going to pitch tomorrow at the meeting, which meant I had a long night ahead of me to know what the issues were that needed to be fixed and how we could market it. I grabbed my notebook and a pen, and started making notes as I skimmed through the pages again. Small issues jumped out, but nothing major. A few scenes needed more exploring, needed more depth to them and I wanted to be in the witness' head more. Minor adjustments, but nothing that required a fix before we could acquire it.

I glanced at my watch and realized my stomach had betrayed me again, letting me forget the time and the fact that I really needed food to survive. I gathered up my laptop and notebook, confident with the notes I had made to write up the report I needed for the morning and ventured inside. The coffee had apparently filled me up enough that I had no idea I hadn't eaten all day and it was now eight p.m. Too late to feel like cooking. My stomach grumbled at the thought of not getting nourishment and I sighed. Take out it would have to be. I had grown so used to ordering out that I often wondered if I remembered how to even cook.

The doorbell ringing pulled my mind from where I was going to eat, straight to annoyance that someone would be bugging me. No one ever showed up here except for Melissa, and even she knew enough to text before just dropping by. I hated surprises. I played with the idea of ignoring it, but when the doorbell was hit again, there was no way I was going to be able to get away with that.

I pulled the door open, ready to blast who was ever on the other side about having no manners showing up late like this and stopped short without a word when Nick stood there smiling, holding a bag of Chinese food.

"Have you eaten?"

I shook my head no, still not finding my voice.

"Didn't think so. You were hard at work it seemed earlier when I walked by and when I went to get the food, you hadn't moved. Did you eat at all today?" Nick rambled on as he stepped into the apartment.

"No, I forgot. Occupational hazard." I smiled.

"Well, Chinese then?" He held out the bag and the aroma had my stomach singing for the smell that wafted out of the bag.

I grabbed it and headed to the kitchen. "Come on in."

Nick followed me into the kitchen, and when I should have been panicking over the fact that I never allow men into my apartment, I was so intrigued that this man had brought me food instead of chastising me for not eating, that I was solely focused on eating. I grabbed two forks and gestured to the table. "Unless you want to go out on the balcony."

"Here's good. You probably could use a change in scenery." He waited until I had sat down before he sat, triggering in me that he had done the same thing at dinner last night. A gentleman through and through. "What were you working on today that had you so engrossed you couldn't think to eat?"

"I work for a publishing house. Reading a new manuscript that I would like to pitch to the team tomorrow morning about acquiring. I had to finish it and then go back through to come up with what issues the books has, what kind of marketing it would require, that kind of stuff." I shrugged like it was no big deal as I shoveled Lo-Mein into my mouth.

"Interesting job you have." Nick pushed the boneless spareribs my way. I helped myself to them and grinned at him. "Found your weakness, have I?"

"Food. Yes, I like food when I haven't eaten all day." I laughed. "But the question is will you always know what kind of food to bring me?"

I swallowed hard as I heard the words come out of my mouth. Even as I joked, I realized it sounded like he would be sticking around.

"I'm not sure it would matter if you hadn't eaten."

"Maybe not." I pushed my plate aside. I had my fill for the moment. At least my stomach had quieted down.

"Sure you had enough?" Nick picked up the table, setting the dishes in the sink and packing up the food to put away in the fridge.

"Yes, thank you."

He turned and leaned against the counter. "You're welcome."

I played with my glass, turning in around and around. I couldn't read Nick. He was comfortable in his own skin and yet, he was unreadable about what his intentions were or what he wanted from me. It made me on edge and I immediately starting thinking of ways to get him to leave.

"Come on." He reached out his hand and led me to the living room. Pulling me down beside him on the couch, he held me close. "Don't overthink it, Izzy."

"Overthink what?" I tried to move away, but he held me close, although I had the impression that if I pushed hard enough he would let me go.

"Whatever it is your overthinking. It was dinner and some quiet time, that's all. I'll leave whenever you are ready for me to go."

I started to protest, but then just closed my mouth and leaned against him. I was rigid and unable to relax, but Nick didn't say a word. He was letting everything be on my terms. What was wrong with him? I mentally laughed at myself. Let yourself go, I berated myself. Don't mess this up. It's just an evening, but I couldn't relax. I sat against him, rigid as a board trying to relax and the more I tried, the tenser I got.

Nick relaxed his arm against me, allowing me to sit up next to him, but not against him. "It's impossible for you to relax, really?" He questioned, but there was no accusation in his voice.

"I'm trying, but I'm not used to having people here and…" My voice trailed off as I realized how ridiculous my excuses sounded. "Nick…"

"I'll go. Thanks for letting me enjoy dinner with you."

"I don't want you to go." I blinked as I realized it was true. I didn't want him to leave, not yet.

"What do you want, Izzy?" Nick sat on the edge of the couch watching me.

"I don't know. I'm no good at these things." I wanted to flee, but couldn't. It was time to face my fears.

"And yet you can't just seem to roll with it and see what happens." It was a statement, not a question and he could see right through me, which scared me even more.

"I want to, believe me, I do. It's just not that easy."

"It's not that difficult either. It's as hard as you make it." Nick rose and pulled me to my feet. He pulled me close to him and held me tight. His lips brushed against my temple. "We'll talk later."

As sank into the couch as he walked out the door. Would he just be another to add to the long list of men I had pushed away through my life? He was different and yet, I wasn't. I still held on to the past and couldn't seem to move forward. Where did I draw the line and start living for myself instead of the foolish girl who thought she had no right to live?

sixteen

Thankfully, Monday mornings were crazy busy at work with pitch meetings. I had two pitches to give and Gayle agreed to both. I was excited about both authors, but it then led to a busy afternoon writing letters to the authors, looking at schedules to see what we could do for release dates and start thinking about editing schedules for both books.

I had just gotten up from my desk for the first time in hours to make some coffee when my phone beeped indicating a text message.

Eat something.

I couldn't help but break into a smile. Only Nick would think to send me a text telling me to eat, knowing only too well I hadn't eaten anything all day, but was easily on my fifth cup of coffee.

Does coffee count? I replied.

NO. You can't keep up these hours if you get sick.

I know. ☹

Text me when you leave tonight and I'll bring you dinner. I'm sure you'll still have work to do at home.

No need. I do have to work even after I get home.

There was no further text. Even though I felt uncomfortable with him showing me that he cared, I felt the twang of disappointment when no further text came in. The rest of the day flew by and I appeased my inner rebellion at being told to eat by simply having a candy bar. It was eating, wasn't it? Nick, after all, had not specified what I should eat. I knew it was a weak argument to say the least, but the independent woman in me fought at being told what to do.

By the time the day ended, I was exhausted and in no way wanting company. Gayle had talked me into actually taking the night off after the hours I had put in during the day and the amount accomplished. I warmed at the quick email I received from Gayle earlier stating simply *Best decision I made to hire you.* Compliments were few and far between with Gayle. You knew she was pleased if nothing was said. And if she was displeased with your work, you knew that also.

Setting caution aside, I sent a quick text to Nick stating I was leaving work and lo and behold I was taking the night off. If nothing else we could enjoy dinner if he was willing. By the time, I left work thirty minutes later, there still hadn't been a reply from Nick and I just knew I had ticked him off earlier by stating he didn't need to bring dinner. Men could be so unreadable and in a world where I read everything and prided myself on knowing the underlying current of things, I was mystified when it came to Nick.

Today had not been the day to wear three-inch heels. My feet were killing me. I kicked of the shoes and grabbing them by the heels, I took the stairs two at a time to the apartment. I stopped short when there in front of my door was a single yellow rose laying across the welcome mat.

As I picked it up, I inhaled the rich scent that took me back to my grandmother's rose garden. Roses were always my favorite. I would spend time with my grandmother as she tended to her roses. The bench in the middle of her rose garden had become my spot. Closing my eyes for a moment, I could see her tanned hands gently deadheading the stems while I talked up a storm to her. She had been the one person I could ever open up to. A pang of despair shot threw me as it always did when I was missing something familiar.

"I wasn't sure if you were a fan of roses or not, but I took a chance." Nick's voice from behind caught me off guard and I swung around to face him.

"Yellow roses are actually my favorite." I smiled, suddenly feeling very shy.

He held up a grocery bag. "Dinner?"

"What is it?" I was leery of the grocery bag. I was in no mood to have to cook a meal, which must have shown clear as day on my face.

"You don't have to cook, don't worry." Nick gestured to the door and I unlocked it and stepped in ahead of him. I dropped my shoes and purse next to the door and started to the kitchen for a vase for the rose.

Nick unpacked the bag. I peeked over his shoulder to see what it was. He was quick though and blocked my view. "Don't you want to go read a manuscript or something?" He snickered.

"Nope. I'm taking the night off. Two of my pitches

were given the go ahead today to acquire. I'll be working my ass off come editing time for these two, but tonight I'm celebrating."

"Good for you. That's a rarity for you."

"Don't think you know me that well." I laughed as he knew exactly how much of a workaholic I was. I leaned against the table and watched him work. Obviously, we weren't having anything hot, but he definitely knew his way around a kitchen. Without asking where things were, he had no problem locating plates and silverware.

"Wine or a beer?" I asked as I crossed the kitchen to the fridge to grab the bottle of white wine.

"Beer if you have it."

I reached in for a Corona and the container of lime wedges already cut. By the time I had poured my glass of wine and prepared his Corona with lime in it, Nick had dinner on the table. The plates were loaded with salad fixings as well as grilled chicken. There was a jar of a creamy herb and yogurt dressing.

"Wow. Nice. I rarely eat healthy and that looks delicious." I tore into it, realizing that the candy bar I had earlier was long gone.

"You didn't eat earlier, did you?" Nick shook his head as he watched me shovel the food into my mouth.

"I did." I mumbled with my mouth full, nodding my head.

"What?"

I swallowed and grinned. "A candy bar."

"A what?" Nick sat back and stared at me. The disbelief on his face made me choke as I took a sip of wine.

"You heard me."

With a last shake of his head, he started eating. We ate in a comfortable silence. There had never been this comfort level with anyone else before. I had always kept my distance from letting someone sit in the coziness of my kitchen. It seemed so intimate. Most men I used just for sex. They could come over, but as soon as the sex was over they were expected to leave. Never were they allowed to share the night with me.

Nick was different. In my gut, I knew that this… whatever this was…was rare and I struggled with how to handle it. It was a craving I desperately wanted, but knew it would end badly. Someone so broken can't function in normalcy. I was so lost in my thoughts, I didn't realize Nick was done eating and was leaned back drinking his beer just watching me.

"You okay?"

I nodded. "Just lost in thought. Occupational hazard." Oh, it was so easy to use work as an excuse for everything.

He cocked his head to the side, but didn't say a word. He drained his beer and reached to pick up the plates.

"Let me clean up. You brought dinner so it's the least I can do." I waved his hands away. "Besides, it's my house."

Nick shrugged. "I'm not expecting you to wait on me."

"Oh, but it's okay that you wait on me in my own house. You want to do something, help yourself to another beer and refill my glass."

The kitchen was clean in short work and we made our way to the balcony. The salt air was heavy in the air with the cloud cover. The sky was dark over the ocean indicative of a storm brewing. I inhaled deeply. No matter how long I had lived here, I would never get sick of the effect the salt air and sound of the waves had on me. I refused to live anywhere but on the ocean. It would kill me if I ever had to move. The ocean was my soul mate.

I don't know how it started, but I'm pretty sure a

bottle of wine later and who knows how many beers Nick had had, but suddenly the friendly banter had turned to more suggestive talk. Nick never made a move to touch me and I had pretty much spelt out to him that I was needing to feel him. It was like a torturous game he was playing, creating anticipated and prolonged foreplay. I was wound tightly and needed release. I know he knew it. I could tell by the way his lips curled up in a half smile.

"You know you have to work tomorrow." Nick changed the subject, dousing me with cold water as those words washed over me.

I nodded, watching him. I didn't want him to go and he didn't appear to be in any hurry to leave. He reached out his foot and laid it against mine, rubbing slowly back and forth. The touch was so light, yet ignited a fire that had been a spark for too many hours now. I sighed. My eyes never left his. I was powerless to move even though I wanted to go straddle him and see how much resolve he really had.

His touch on my foot was not enough. I ached to feel his hands on me, his mouth. A soft sigh escaped me and he chuckled. "You're doing it on purpose!" The words were out before I thought about it.

"Doing what?"

"Don't be coy with me." I rose, took two steps and positioned myself in front of him. I stood completely still, waiting.

Nick, with one hand, reached for me. I was still in my dress, having not bothered to change when I got home. He slid his hand up my thigh under the dress. Stopping mid-thigh, he hooked my leg and pulled me closer, throwing me off balance. I caught myself with my knee in his chair, and straddled his lap. Moving to adjust myself for comfort, I felt the proof that he was wound just as tight as I was.

Our lips met, and I no longer could tell who was in control, but I relinquished any sense of control I thought I had as he thoroughly kissed me. His tongue stroked mine and with every stroke, the fire within flamed higher until I was moaning softly against his lips as my hips were moving in a slow rhythm against him.

He pulled back and looked into my eyes. "Are you sure you want this, Izzy?"

"Yes, very much so." I stood and reached out a hand to him, as he stood I led him to the bedroom.

Once inside the bedroom, he took total control and all I could do was melt. He peeled off my dress over my head and with a quick hand, undid my bra. Before I could take a deep breath, I stood naked before him with his hands wandering over my body. I pulled his t-shirt over his head and helped him unzip his jeans, pushing them down so he was free of all clothing also. I reached for him and stroked him until he was trembling. He reached for my hand and pulled it off him, guiding me backward towards the bed.

As the back of my knees hit the bed, I fell backwards, pulling Nick with me. I squirmed, trying to get him to enter me, but he kept pulling back. He pushed my hands above my head and placed gentle kisses down my jawline. I moaned in frustration as he chuckled softly. "I'm not rushing, Izzy. Enjoy the ride."

The next thing I knew he was making his way down my body. His lips grasped my nipple and sucked hard, eliciting a moan from me as I arched my back to give him greater access. He switched to the other breast and sucked hard again, his fingers rolling my other nipple. I ground my hips against him moaning, my eyes closed trying to hold on as I throbbed in wanting agony.

He continued to kiss his way down my belly, kissing first the inside of my right thigh and then the left. I could feel his breath on me and I squirmed trying to make contact with him. He pulled back and caressed my thighs with just enough pressure that I couldn't move. His hands moved to grab firmly to my hips to hold me in place.

"Nick, please." I softly begged.

I felt his tongue gently run along me, stopping on my sweet spot and staying there. He sucked gently, increasing in pressure and suction until I could take no more. I was powerless under his grip on my hips and I moaned in frustration, begging him to bring me to climax. I was on the edge and yet, Nick backed off slightly, his tongue wandering round my wetness, probing in and out of me, until I settled a bit.

Once settled, he attacked again with deliberateness and within seconds I was crying out his name and careening over the edge of oblivion. Once the trembling stopped and I had a moment to catch my breath, Nick moved back up my body and as he kissed me deeply, he slid his hardness deep within me thrusting hard. I matched his paced, thrust for thrust, until he could no longer hold off and filled me with his release.

I lay holding him, trying to calm my breathing against his shoulder. He pulled out and rolled over, holding me close as he moved. I pushed against him and whispered, "Bathroom". As I came out of the bathroom, I realized Nick was settled in for the night. Panic gripped me. I never allowed a man to spend the night with me. Sex was great, but holding me through the night was a level of intimacy I never wanted...couldn't afford to take on.

I climbed into bed and lay rigidly beside him. He turned towards me and ran his fingers down my belly. "You want me to leave, don't you?"

"I have an early morning tomorrow." I tried to sound disappointed, but Nick saw right through it.

"What you need is to allow someone to just be there for you. You need to be held and instead you push everyone away." Nick rolled me on my side away from him and spooned up close to me. I felt him pull me in close, so I'm nestled right against him. He wrapped his arms around me and kissed the back of my neck.

"Izzy, go to sleep. Let me just keep you safe tonight."

I couldn't help myself. The massive adrenalin let down from the multiple orgasms and the warmth of him close to me, shut my eyes on their own.

Before I knew it, I had for the first time fallen asleep in a man's arms.

seventeen

The alarm woke me with a start. Five a.m. I groaned inwardly and realized the warmth of Nick's body snuggled close to me had kept me from my usual out of bed before the alarm routine. I snuck my hand out from under the covers to shut it off. As I tried to move slowly out from under his arm, my mind whirled with how to get Nick out of here so I could get ready for work.

He groaned and rolled over, leaving me free to get out of bed. I stared at him for a moment, taking the time while his eyes were closed to admire his features. The softness of his face while sleeping. His tousled hair brought an innocent look to him. I watched as his mouth turned into a smile, eyes still closed.

"Like what you see?" He rolled towards me and held out his hand.

"Get up." I turned and hurried from the bedroom. I couldn't fall back into bed with this man. I had already let my guard down and allowed him to hold me all night… and how I had enjoyed it.

Starting the coffeemaker, I processed the impact of allowing Nick to spend the night. This was a level of intimacy I never allowed myself and wasn't sure how I felt about it. I shook my thoughts clear and turned my attention to my work day. Better to dive into work mode than think about Nick. He was too damn distracting for my own good.

As I headed into the adjoining bathroom to shower and saw he was lying in bed, hands behind his head just waiting for me to return. I smiled at him, but continued without saying a word into the bathroom. Blasting the hot water, I brushed my teeth before jumping into the shower. The heat soothed my nerves as I shampooed my hair. I sighed deeply allowing the hot water to rain down on me, washing the stress and anxiety of this newfound experience before me.

By the time, I had dried off and returned to the bedroom, the bed was empty and made.

Nick was nowhere to be found.

Had he pulled a run out the door without saying goodbye? Part of me was in denial that he would do that and the other part prayed he had so I wouldn't have to face my fears of dealing with the "morning after" awkwardness. I dressed quickly and refocused on work and mentally prioritized the work that needed to be done.

I was putting in my earrings as I moved into the kitchen to fix my coffee and grab my stuff to get to the office quickly. I was already in my mind preparing emails that would need to go out. I stopped short when I entered the kitchen and there was Nick, sipping a cup of coffee, leaning against the counter.

I smiled hesitantly. "Morning."

He grinned over his coffee. "This is killing you, isn't it?"

I shook my head no. "I have no idea what you are talking about."

He pointed to my travel mug sitting next to the coffeemaker. "It's all ready so you can make a quick getaway."

I couldn't hold the laughter back any more. "Is it that obvious?"

Nick pulled me into his arms and kissed me softly. "I get it. Don't worry."

What I couldn't fathom was a man actually getting me not wanting the cuddling and being clingy to him. This was a man that understood the meaning of space, although last night he hadn't forced me to allow him to stay, yet he knew it wasn't the comfort zone I was used to.

Nick broke through my thoughts. "You should get to work." He handed me my travel mug and headed to the door.

I stood there for a moment, mug in hand staring after him. I grabbed my bag and followed him out the door, locking it behind me. "Have a good day." I gave him a kiss and we started down the stairs of the building together. There was no awkwardness as we parted and went our separate ways to work. My mind was already focused on work and the day ahead.

The day flew by as I engrossed myself in work, emails and setting up editing schedules for my new acquisitions. Before I realized it, the day was coming to an end and thoughts of the night before had yet to surface in my mind…until I got closer to leaving work. My mind ran the gamut of wondering if Nick would show up tonight or if I would not hear from him again. Did I want to hear from him? Or did I continue to resist the level of intimacy he wanted? It scared the hell out of me to think I would even be capable of anything along the sex without strings relationship…if you could call that a relationship. Intimacy was something I gave up a long time ago when I pushed Jack away.

I sighed as I pushed back away from my desk and shut down the computer. I had another manuscript to read over and I would rather do it at home on the balcony with a glass of wine than here at the office. Not that I was leaving the office at a reasonable hour a glance to my watch told me -- seven o'clock already. I would be another late night.

Disappointment hit me like a punch to the gut when I arrived at the apartment. The house seemed lonely tonight after having dinner and spending the evening last night with Nick. The question of "what did I really want" played through my head as I heated left overs and poured a glass of wine. I left the microwave running as I went into the bedroom to change into my comfort clothes, an oversized t-shirt and sweatpants. I looked at the bed and heat flooded me as the memories of sex with Nick came to mind. I could feel my cheeks flush at the vivid memories that played through my mind.

The beep of the microwave pulled me from the memories and I turned away. This bed would never be the same again for me. Another sigh escaped me as I headed for the kitchen. One night was all it was. I hadn't even heard from him today and that was typical and usually what I wanted from men. It was easier to have sex, send them on their way and get on with my life than the level of intimacy I shared with Nick last night. It was great and

I had enjoyed the warmth of his body next to mine for the night much more than I would ever admit, but it was distracting to my career to allow that to continue.

Steeling my emotions once more, I grabbed my dinner and my laptop and headed for the balcony. Reading for the night would certainly put me back into 24/7 work mode that I had become accustomed to.

eighteen

I stared at myself in the mirror. Contact with Nick during the week had been sporadic, but there just enough to let me know he was still around. And yet here I was dressing to go to a party with him tonight. My blue jean capris and a jade colored blouse gave the impression of nice, but casual. Nick had been vague about the type of people that would be there, just that they were going to a friend's house and it would be mostly business associates.

Business networking I could do. It allowed me to slip into my work persona and be more extroverted than I felt. I was just finishing putting on my mascara when the doorbell rang. I took a deep breath to calm my fluttering stomach as I thought of Nick. There was no doubt I was attracted to him.

Pulling the door open, I smiled when I saw him. God,

I loved to see him in a blue shirt. It just made his blue eyes pop. I gestured him to come in. "Got to grab my shoes."

I made a beeline for the bedroom to find my shoes and give myself a minute to gather my wits. I hadn't expected the surge of heat in me just at the sight of him again. Calming my thought process, I avoided looking at the bed knowing full well memories would not help me to get myself together before going back out to him.

"You ready?" Nick called from the living room.

"Yup." I slipped on my sandals and entered to finding him leaning against the door. "Don't act like I kept you waiting for hours."

He grinned and opened the door. We rode in silence to the party. I kept myself from letting my nerves take over, watching the landscape go by. The driveway, when we arrived, was full of cars.

"A small party, huh?"

"It's just a few people really. Trust me, you will enjoy these people."

I nodded. "Are they all people you work with?"

"No. Friends of friends, people from various networking groups. It's not about business tonight though and they are just people who have come to enjoy each other's company."

I walked beside him to the front door and took comfort when he entwined his fingers with mine and the small squeeze he gave my hand. The door was flung open by a man I could only describe as a giant. He filled the door frame, beer in one hand, laughing at something being said just before opening the door.

"Hey, man. Come on in." He stepped aside as we moved into the foyer of the house. I glanced around and people were milling around talking in groups.

"Vince, this is Isabelle. Isabelle, Vince." I reached out a hand and found myself being pulled into a bear hug.

"Any friend of Nick's is a friend of mine. Come on it." He let me go abruptly as he pulled me into the hug, yet keeping his arm around my shoulders and turning me towards the crowd. He propelled me forward through the throng of people towards the kitchen. "Beverages are in here. Help yourself."

Before I knew it, he had disappeared and Nick and I were standing in the kitchen looking at each other. He handed me a bottled wine cooler and grabbed a beer. "Shall we?"

I nodded. The cool bottle in my hand gave me focus beyond my nerves of meeting all these new people. *Treat it like work.* I held on to that thought as Nick brought me around to different groups and introduced me. God, I hope there wasn't a quiz later as names escaped me as soon as I was introduced to people.

Finally, Nick got trapped by a group of men and started talking sports. I drifted over to a quiet corner to find a place to sit. I had long since finished my drink, but continued to hold the empty bottle just to keep my hands busy. A sigh of relief escaped me as I sank into a chair and just sat back to take in the scene. I never had been a "middle of the party" type of person and much preferred being on the outskirts just watching.

"Can I join you?" A petite woman with blond hair pulled back in a ponytail was standing next to the chair next to me.

"Please."

"I don't know about you, but I really hate these gatherings. Don't get me wrong, I love talking with people, but I prefer a smaller group."

"I totally agree. I'm only here because Nick insisted we come. Not usually my scene."

"I'm Diane."

"Isabelle. Nice to meet you."

I searched the group for Nick. He was still in the same group of men, laughing and having a good time. It wasn't that I was not having a good time, but if I was being honest, I was ready to go home. A couple of hours of this was enough.

"Are you Nick's new girlfriend?" Diane's question cut through my thoughts and I glanced over at her.

"Girlfriend? Well…I would say we're friends."

"Really? When I heard he was bringing a girl with him, I just figured it was a girlfriend. He never brings anyone to these gatherings. Last time it someone he was seriously dating, so I figured…" Diane shrugged her shoulders.

I watched her and tried to read her facial expressions, which were completely neutral. Did he consider her his girlfriend? "I don't know if I would go that far. We've gone out a couple of times."

Diane was trying to read me, I knew it. I had done the same thing to her and yet irritation grew in me that this girl would be trying to figure me out. Immediately I reinforced my wall of protection, becoming more unreadable. It didn't seem to faze Diane in the least. "Well, welcome to the group regardless. I take comfort in the fact that you are here and we can sit in the corner together so I don't look quite so unsociable."

Despite myself, I felt relief. She wasn't prying, just making conversation. "What do you do?"

"For work?" Diane seemed surprised I would ask.

I nodded.

"I do some life coaching mostly, privately and I work

some with high school seniors as they try to figure out what they want in life."

"That sounds interesting." I had no clue what life coaching entailed, but it sounds lighthearted and fun.

"How about you?" Diane asked.

"Junior editor at a publishing house."

"Wow. You get to read books before they are bought and decide if they get published or not?"

I nodded. "That's part of it. It's long hours and a lot of reading, but I love it."

"I'm sure. Must leave you very little time for a social life."

"Yeah, not much of a social life, but I'm okay with that."

"Really? I think I would die if I didn't have friends that I could talk to once in a while, and you know a guy that you can have around at least sporadically." She winked giving me that you know what I mean look.

I chuckled. "Exactly, but life is what you make of it and right now I'm focusing on my career. I don't need the hassle of any outside pressure at this point."

The smile faded from Diane's face. "Hassle?"

"Well, you know what I mean. I work long hours, I don't want to have to try and pacify a man that can't handle an independent woman."

"Hmmm, well, I'm sure Nick understands that." She was invasive in her comment and for some reason it jabbed me straight in the heart. Did I really give her the impression that I could care less about Nick or his feelings? Was it any of her business? I bristled inwardly at the thought that someone would care whether Nick and I were actually in a relationship and what kind of relationship that was.

It was like she could read my mind when I heard her next words. "Don't let my comments bother you." And yet those words alone bothered me the most.

"Not at all. Most people don't understand someone else's life because they don't know the details of it." I tried valiantly to portray the bravado that I was not feeling.

"Isabelle, I didn't mean to offend you. We've all walked different paths that have brought us to where we are. There is no right or wrong paths to take in life."

I almost choked on my snort at her words. "No right or wrong path?" The bitter laugh I gave probably said more about me than I wanted, but I didn't care. "Some people wouldn't agree with that."

"No, they probably wouldn't, but they are probably the ones, like my parents, who feel their children can never do anything right."

Ah, a kindred spirit. Maybe she wasn't judging me, but could honestly relate to the way I felt about life and relationships. I shrugged, the neutral persona falling back into place. We fell into a comfortable silence, each perusing the room. I searched for Nick. He had moved from the group and I no longer saw him. A flash of panic set in.

"Okay, I'm dying to know. How did you meet Nick? He is the hottest catch around and yet remains so elusive, really staying out of relationships." Diane broke through my thoughts.

I smiled at the memory. "Apparently unbeknownst to me, we shared a favorite spot at the beach. He found me there and not expecting it, he dropped his coffee. It certainly wasn't the most pleasant meeting. Boy, can he be cranky when he doesn't have coffee." I chuckled.

Diane was staring at me, mouth slightly ajar. "He

dropped his coffee? Yeah, I have seen him without coffee. Lucky you survived."

"It killed him that I was sitting there drinking my coffee and I have to say, I probably rubbed that in a bit." I paused. "You know he probably is elusive because he doesn't like to be chased."

"Is that your professional opinion or a personal one?"

I shrugged. "Just a thought."

Diane nodded. "Sounds like you speak from experience."

"No, not me. I'm not one someone chases after."

"No? You have to know you are a very beautiful woman, Isabelle. You had every woman in this room wondering and immediately jealous."

I raised my eyebrow at her. "I can't imagine why. I'm just an ordinary person who has become a workaholic."

"And that is the most dangerous type of beauty… when you don't even realize how extraordinary you are." Diane nodded towards Nick walking towards us. "He knows exactly how beautiful you are, you can see it when he looks at you."

I scoffed. I would never understand other women's way of thinking about the same genre. I seemed to have missed the female gene that made you be jealous of other women because they may be attractive. I could care less what women thought of me or what others did with their lives. I just wanted to live in peace…well, and maybe someday find a contentment with my life that would allow me to finally be happy.

"Hey, I wondered where you disappeared to." Nick squatted next to my chair. "Hi Diane."

"Hey, Nick." Diane stood and held out her card to me. "If you want keep in touch. I enjoyed chatting with you, Isabelle."

"Me too. Thanks." I took her card and glanced down as she walked away. Life coach and counselor. Ahhh, well that made more sense the way she seemed to pry, yet didn't. I slipped the card into the back pocket of my jeans.

"You ready to ditch this place?" Nick stood and shifted into the chair that Diane had vacated.

"Whenever you are."

"Really? You would sit here for another few hours?" Nick's eyes searched mine.

Staying as neutral as possible, I nodded. "If that's what you wanted to do."

"Get real, Izzy. You are uncomfortable with this many people around. Just say it."

I sighed. "I enjoyed talking with Diane. No, I don't really like crowds, but if you are having fun, we can stay."

Nick shook his head at me. "It's not about what I want to do. I want you to be comfortable and say if you're not."

"It's a party, not a life or death situation, Nick. Don't make it more than it is." Irritation ran through me. I hated being put on the spot and hated even more the fact that he seemed to read me better than anyone ever had.

He reached out a hand to me. "Come on."

I took his hand and allowed him to lead me to the front door, saying our good-byes as we weaved our way through the crowd. I glanced at my watch. It was only ten, still early for a Friday night.

nineteen

We climbed the steps to my apartment without speaking. Nick held my hand in his warm one, squeezing it gently every so often. I'm not sure why, but this reassured me and fanned the flame within me that seemed to burn only for him. He stopped at the door, allowing me to unlock it and step in. I turned back when I realized he had stopped right outside the door.

"Aren't you coming in?"

His blue eyes were piercing as he locked his eyes with mine. "I probably shouldn't." Confusion ran through me. I cocked my head at him without saying a word. "Izzy, I'm not going to have sex with you tonight."

"Um, okay." My mind started running through scenarios that over the past few days I had replayed over and over in my mind. What had I done? The sex had been incredible, at least I thought so. Apparently he did not.

"It's not what you need right now." Nick took one step inside the door, but didn't reach for me.

"And you all of a sudden know what I need?" My voice laced with sarcasm startled even me.

"I didn't mean it that way." He sighed and ran his fingers through his hair. "I...I think you need more than you let on and I don't mean sex. You act like you just want the sex without strings, and you seem to think that any guy just wants that too, but I think deep down you truly crave the intimacy you avoid."

I shook my head. "You know nothing about me." I stared him down. The nerve of him.

"Izzy." His soft voice broke through my irritation. "I want that intimacy with you, but I am not going to be another one of your boy toys who you have sex with and then run away from."

"I don't run away." A choked laugh escaped me. "And you think pretty high of yourself if you think you would fall in the category of boy toy. That's an exclusive club." There was no getting through this brick wall now. My defensive barrier was up and there was no way in hell it was coming down around this man again. I mentally berated myself for allowing the slightest thought that Nick would be different than any other man I had encountered.

He leaned against the door frame, silent, waiting for me to say more.

"I guess that says it all." I gestured to the door. "You probably should go now."

"You didn't hear a word I said, did you?" He didn't change his posture and his laid-back attitude was grating on my last nerve.

"I heard you." I turned my back to him, fighting back

the threat of tears filling my eyes. I'd be damned if he saw he had cracked my defense for a second.

"Izzy." The single word, spoken as almost a question, forced me to steel myself and turn towards him.

"Nick, please go."

He shook his head. "Not until you understand what I'm saying."

"For the love of God." I slipped off my sandals and started for the bedroom. Nick didn't move and so I slammed the door behind me and took a deep breath. I heard the apartment door shut and breathed a sigh of relief. I changed into an oversized t-shirt and my sweats. I pulled the bedroom door open and stopped short seeing Nick leaning against the door, waiting for me.

"Are you ready to talk?"

"No. Just leave, Nick." I continued to avoid eye contact and flopped down on the couch.

He strolled over to the couch and knelt down beside me. "Izzy. I want you, more than anything. But I want to hold you when you need it, and through the night. I want to fix your coffee in the morning before you go to work. It's not about the sex. I want more and I don't think you're capable of that right now."

"Right. Poor broken Izzy. So tell me, did you orchestrate this whole meeting tonight between me and Diane hoping I would fall into your arms and tell you how much I need counseling and thank God you were around to show me the way."

"I didn't know Diane was going to be there and no, that thought never crossed my mind that you needed counseling. But here is a news flash for you, we're all broken to some extent. We all have a past that haunts us, but you need to find a way to move past it. Whoever broke your heart, I won't compete with." He stood and stared down at me.

I stood and strode to the door, yanking it open. "I broke my own heart, Nick. And you're right, you can't compete with that."

"Damn it, Izzy. Don't shut me out."

"I'm not. You decided on the rules and I'm just playing by them. You don't want sex. Well then I don't want you here." My voice came out stronger than I felt. I wanted to crumble to a heap on the floor and curse my life. How did I even get to this point?

He kissed me on the cheek as he walked past me. "I'll text you later. Think about the words I actually said to you, Izzy...not what you think you heard." He was gone before I could react and I refrained from slamming the door behind him.

I made my bed, as the saying goes...I sank to a sitting position against the door. I didn't deserve someone like Nick in my life. On some level he reminded me of Jack. Kind and gentle, and I knew at some point there would be hurt in his eyes just like Jack's that last fateful day I had seen him. Tears no longer could flow for my losses. They continued to grow by the day and by now I was immune to the pain they caused. Over the years, I had created the barrier that allowed me to become numb every time a new loss hit me. Nick, just one more loss I could add to the list.

Would Nick have pulled this crap had I not met Diane tonight? Could that truly have been a random meeting that he had no intention of utilizing?

Snap out of it, Isabelle. Do what you do best. I pushed myself up and grabbed my laptop. Thankfully there was always an abundance of work to be done even on a weekend. I threw myself into my work and let time drift away me.

Caught up in a new manuscript, I continued reading until well after two in the morning. When I finally closed my laptop, tiredness hit me. I glanced down at my phone that had been silenced while I was working and there were three missed calls from Nick and a text message.

You okay?

I replied. *Of course. Working like usual. Have a good night.*

I took myself off to bed hoping sleep would overtake me, but as I slipped between the sheets, memories of Nick holding me filled my mind and I tossed and turned. Flopping onto my back for what seemed like the millionth time in the couple of hours I had been in bed, I sighed. I had done this. I knew that. The truth of the matter was I had now allowed myself to be happy ever, not since that fateful day when I had failed at the suicide attempt. Sure, life was better than it had ever been for me, but I still carried the guilt and heartache around with me like a badge of honor.

I was broken. My heart shattered years ago and I had never allowed myself the chance to let it heal. Jack, by now, had the wife he wanted and a family. He had probably pursued his dream in the Air Force and was living his life to the fullest. Because, let's face it, I was not someone that was difficult to get over. I would never leave a lasting impression on anyone and the sooner I realized that, maybe, just maybe, the sooner I would be able to move on with my life.

I rolled to my side. I hated middle of the night epiphanies. They soiled my mood. I kicked back the covers and glanced at the clock. Four a.m. I had been in bed all of two hours and there would be no sleep. I grabbed a sweatshirt and slipped it over my head. Grabbing my phone and my keys, I headed for the door. There was only one place that could help ease the stress I was feeling.

I slipped off my flip flops as soon as I got to the water's edge. I was headed to the rocks, my favorite place to sit and think, but right now I needed to breathe the salt air and feel the cool water on my feel to ground me. I walked slowly, kicking my feet a little bit with each step to watch the spray of water fall just in front of me. I allowed the coolness on my feet to soothe the mood swings inside of me. I inhaled the salt air and let it fill my lungs, the heady scent bringing my memories to a happier time.

I grew up spending summer days at the beach along the coast of Maine. These were my happy memories. Ones that I leaned on to bring me back from the dark edge and the thoughts that still plagued me of how much better I would be if I just let go of trying to live this life. Thoughts that I had battled for years and only once acted on. Even after that day, I battled to just live each day. Sure there were moments when I found myself being happy and successful, but they were long lasting. They were never what I craved when I thought of contentment.

Nick had hit it right on the head tonight when he said I craved intimacy. It was the one thing I feared the most as it was the thing that could destroy me. I found myself at the rocks and climbed over to my favorite spot. I settled in and closed my eyes. The sound of the waves crashing against the rocks washed the stress from my neck and shoulders.

My phone vibrated in my hand. It was too early on a Saturday to be work.

You awake?

Nick. I sighed. I wanted nothing more than to avoid

him and I could ignore it under the pretense of sleeping, but if he was texting me, he already knew I was awake.

Yeah. What's up?

I'm sorry for earlier.

I sighed. *No worries.*

I sat there staring at my phone, wanting to hear from him, yet wanting to distance myself even further.

We need to talk about this.

Communication was not my strong suit and immediately the stress relief I had found here at the beach was gone at the thought of talking about the past and how much of it I may have to reveal to him.

Right this second? I followed it with a smiley face, hoping he would take it as a joke and not as the stall tactic it was.

Over coffee?

I haven't slept at all tonight. I really need to crash. It wasn't a lie. I was exhausted. With a sigh, I pushed myself off the rocks and headed for home.

You're not going to sleep. We both know it.

The simple text held a ton of truth it in and I hated that he knew me that well already. The real crux of the matter was I would sleep, if he was holding me and that fact alone had me running for the hills, scared to death. I was dragging ass by the time I got back to my apartment and started up the stairs. I hadn't answered Nick and I prayed he would just let it go and give me space, which also equated to the fact that if he gave me space, I knew he was walking away. My nonsensical logic always brought a smile to my face.

Yet, my feet slowed as I neared the top of the stairs. My kind of logic never worked for me. It led me down paths that ultimately were bad decisions. Or, so I thought.

Maybe it was the nonsensical thought process that led me to bad decisions. Sleep deprivation definitely made my thought process sketchy at best. I needed to sleep off this fog of depression that had overcome me tonight.

twenty

A few hours of sleep had done wonders for my mood. Sitting on the balcony after my nap, enjoying another cup of coffee, I stared at my phone. I had never answered Nick hours previously when he texted me. I knew the conversation was looming over us, but I just didn't want to deal with it.

Avoidance. That was my specialty. After all, hadn't I started my journey down the path of relationships just that way – never talking to Jack about what was going on? The hurt in Jack's eyes still haunted me even after all these years. True the pain lessened a bit with time for myself, but I would never get over him. I just couldn't bring myself to put myself out there with another man and risk breaking my heart all over again. Sex without strings was much easier to deal with. No intimacy, no conversations regarding misunderstandings. But I had broken that rule the minute I allowed Nick to spend the night with me.

I felt the blackness of depression hover above me. I was walking a thin line, jumping back and forth over that line, between sanity and clarity to depression and illogical thoughts. For years I had battled depression. There were moments that I just couldn't get myself out of bed. Days where I just wanted to curl up and die. I had made myself a promise that I would never go down that road again, but damn it was hard to hold on sometimes to the clarity that kept the darkness away.

I needed more. I knew that. My heart ached with the constant solitude and impending future alone. Dysfunction was second nature to me and never through there would be a chance that I would experience anything different. I had fought the darkness since I was in junior high. It was life...or so I thought. Could I live differently? Would I ever be rid of the black cloud over me?

Diane came to mind. She knew Nick and I didn't want to open up too much about myself to her, but my mind circled back to her name. I was so guarded when getting to know someone. No one knew the internal battle I fought every day just to have the will to carry on. Maybe just having a girlfriend would help. God knows I was alone all the time. I never went out, but I knew what I was signing up for when I agreed to the job. Eighty hours a week most weeks and I loved my job, but as each year went by I had the nagging feeling there was something missing in my life.

I could close my eyes and be that eighteen-year-old sitting in her room, taking pill after pill, trying to ease the pain again. The memory was so vivid. It would never be erased from my mind. No one understood that. The pain and anguish I had been feeling that made me think there had been no other option but try to escape it. I had failed. How many more years could I beat myself up for it? I had never forgiven myself for the failure. I chuckled. To this day, I consider the attempt a failure, but I couldn't forgive myself for the failure, but it never crossed my mind to forgive myself for the feelings of depression, for letting Jack down and pushing him away.

It still felt like a knife to my heart every time I thought of Jack. I had been so in love with him.

Sighing, I drained my coffee. I needed a new adventure. Shopping the pier was always different and it would get me out of the house at least for a little while.

As I wandered along the pier, in and out of shops, my mind cleared. I could play the tourist. Picking up a cute beach bag, I looked at the price tag. Sale.

"Nice bag." I turned and came face to face with Diane.

"Hi." I held up the bag. "Nothing beats a sale."

"No kidding. I love coming to the pier to check things out." Diane started rifling through the t-shirt rack.

My mind reeled. Here was my chance to maybe pick her brain, but how to do that without sounding completely insane.

We shifted through racks of sale items, only an occasional word spoken. The sense of walking on eggshells prevailed and I was ready to go home. I was too exhausted to try and be politically correct.

"Let's get a drink and chat." Diane broke through my mental stressing.

"Sure." I made my purchases and met her at the front of the store. "Where to?"

"There is the Flamingo Bar right up the pier. How's that?"

"Sounds good." My mind reeled with what we could possibly talk about. Thinking she was a life coach was totally different than thinking she was a counselor, and for some reason it grated on me to think of talking to her, friend or not...although just meeting someone hardly constituted being friends.

"What's going on in that mind?" Diane settled into an outside table.

"I don't know. Should there be something in particular?"

"Ahhh." Diane nodded. "You've got that wall up because you realize I'm a counselor and now you're afraid to just talk to me."

A waitress appeared at our table and we both ordered a Margarita. With a deep breath, I started to deny it, but then shook my head. "Yeah, that's about it."

"That's why I tell people I'm a life coach, and really it's the same thing." Diane sat back and looked out over the ocean. "I really just thought we could be friends, never gave it a thought that my profession would freak you out."

"Just to clarify, I'm not freaked out." I made a face at her. "I've been trying to work through some stuff and it just caught me by surprise."

We sat in silence until our drinks appeared in front of us. Diane held up her drink. "A toast, to new beginnings and good friends." We clinked glasses and took a drink.

"I want to know about Nick. Come on, details." Diane sat forward.

Laughter erupted from me. It had been years since I had a girlfriend to confide in. "Not much to tell really."

"Pfft. Don't believe it."

"Nick's a great guy. I'm just not sure we're looking for the same things." I drank my drink a little too fast, avoidance at its finest.

"What's not to want? Have you seen that rock-hard

ass, his pecs…hell, his whole body?" Diane stared at me, waiting for an answer.

Heat flooded my face.

"Oh, you have…and I'm thinking by the degree of that blush, you've seen him naked. Good for you."

"Oh, my God. Are you kidding me?" I tried to choke back the laughter, but Diane was sitting there fanning herself making swooning faces. "Knock it off. He's not a sex object…or so he tells me."

"Wait. He told you he wasn't a sex object. Give… there's a story there."

I downed the rest of my drink in a single swallow and sat back in the chair. "He wants more than I can give."

"More than sex?"

"Yup, an actual relationship and I just can't do that. It's against my DNA to actually be in a relationship."

"Hmmm." Diane stared off at the ocean again.

"Don't psychoanalysis me."

"I'm not. But I do have to question whether you can't or just won't?"

I shrugged. "Doesn't matter. It's the same end result."

"I'm thinking you got your heart broke pretty bad at some point." Diane gestured to the waitress for another round. "We all have."

"Well do tell about your heartbreak then. Anything to get off the subject of me." I watched Diane carefully. She wasn't guarded, and seemed like an open book, but there had to be taboo conversations with her. Even girl-friends kept somethings to themselves.

"For me, the love of my life left me when I put my career first. I didn't realize what I was doing until it was too late. About five years ago now. I go out some, but no one compares to Patrick. I find myself in an endless cycle of comparing everyone to him, knowing they won't measure up." She chuckled. "I have a feeling you and I have walked fairly similar lives, maybe not in the same circumstances, but the same outcomes."

I nodded, but said nothing.

"What kind of stuff are you trying to work through? I don't want to pry and I'm not counseling you."

"Just stuff. I'm a workaholic and proud to admit that. I have moved up the ladder at work quicker than anyone else, but I put in the eighty hours a week to do it." I paused. "It gets lonely at times, but that's the price for a career, right?"

"Amen, sister."

"Speaking of work, I do have some to finish up before Monday and I didn't sleep well last night." I stood and put enough cash on the table to cover our drinks.

"Too much." Diane pointed to the money and reached for her wallet.

"You can get next time. I did enjoy this. Thanks."

"You've got my card. Get in touch when you're ready to get together."

I nodded before walking off. I strolled down the broad walk and onto the beach. As I slipped off my flip-flops, I allowed the warm sand to calm my nerves. I liked Diane and could probably become friends with her, but there still was that whole counselor thing getting in the way. Damn, I needed to clear my head of Nick, or Jack. Sigh. Jack. My heart still ached with the thought of him, more so with a couple of drinks.

twenty-one

Sunday morning came as I sat on the balcony watching the ocean. I had been sitting there all night. Feelings of unworthiness and no self-worth had rolled over me like a steam roller last night and I had polished off a bottle of Jameson. The bright sun danced off the waves, torturing my eyes.

Fear gripped me at the thought of closing my eyes. I wouldn't allow myself to go to sleep. My dreams of Jack were so vivid, the hurt in his blue eyes, the pain of my heart shattering. The reality of the situation was staring me in the face and I just couldn't accept it. This wasn't about Jack or Nick. It was about me. Plain and simple. It was me who had screwed up most of my life and it was me that was constantly shutting everyone out of my life. When did it end? When would I be courageous enough to face the truth and just deal with it?

I picked up my phone and stared at it. Inhaling deeply, I poised my fingers above the keyboard, waiting. Waiting for what? *Just do it, Isabelle.* I gave myself the mental kick in the ass I needed and typed out the text.

Meet me at the rocks?

I stood and went inside. Filling my water bottle and gulping down two ibuprofen, I put my sunglasses on and headed to the rocks without any answer. I feared and hoped simultaneously that Nick would show up. My throat was parched from the effects of drinking so much the night before and yet no matter how much water I drank, the thirst was not quenched. This had to stop. No more self-medicating and no more denial.

I sat at the rocks waiting for Nick. He had not responded to the text message. I had been waiting about twenty minutes and still no sign of him. I checked my phone again for the hundredth time in the last minute. Still nothing. I sipped my water and sat back against the rock. Closing my eyes, I allowed the sounds of the waves to soothe my nerves. I drifted off to a brief slumber, the water sounding more distant as I drifted away. I wasn't in a deep enough sleep that I startled when I felt him sit down next to me. He didn't say a word, yet I knew it was him.

I opened one eye to see him. He was staring off to the ocean, sitting leaning forward with his hands clenched together. My heart cracked just a little. This weekend hadn't been easy on him either obviously, but this was his doing. I closed my eye again. It wasn't his doing. It was my own and I knew it, but how do you explain that to someone else.

"Hey." I spoke softly. "I'm glad you came."

"Yup, I'm here. What's up?" His voice was cold, and he couldn't completely hide his hurt from my ears. I wanted to scream at him.

"You said we needed to talk."

"Yup, yesterday and you never answered me." Nick leaned back against the rock and glanced over at me.

"I'm sorry." I closed my eyes again.

"I wasn't trying to hurt you, Izzy."

"I know and it's not you. Nick, it is all me." I sighed. "In case you didn't notice, I'm pretty screwed up."

Nick laughed, if you could call it that. "We all are screwed up, Izzy. You hold on to it like a shield, deflecting everyone away from you."

I turned to face him. "I don't know how to fix this. I don't even know…"

"I think you do, but you're just too scared for whatever reason."

"I don't even know what I want in life, Nick, not beyond work." I fought to keep the tears from falling. Exhaustion had made me emotional and I hated showing any part of that vulnerability to someone.

"Don't you?" He shrugged and after a brief pause, "maybe you don't."

"I'm afraid." The words were barely a whisper and I prayed he hadn't heard the admission. He wrapped his arm around me and pulled me closer.

"You're not alone, Izzy." He kissed my forehead. "Find a way to face your fears. I'm not going anywhere. If nothing else, you have my friendship."

The words registered in my mind…words I wanted to hear from someone else for years. I was not alone in being afraid, not alone. The worst thing about depression is feeling like no one else could possibly feel what you are feeling. And sitting there with Nick's arms around me, the tears finally fell. Tears I couldn't hold back any longer. I was beyond hurt and afraid, I was still living in guilt from the past, unable to forgive myself. Years of pretending I was fine had finally all come to a head and I couldn't hide behind the pretense of being strong any longer.

I leaned against Nick and absorbed the strength he freely gave. I had no idea how I was going to fix this...or my life moving forward, but at least I was finally ready to admit I needed to fix it.

"Talk to me." Nick's voice was soft.

I took a deep breath and exhaled slowly. "What do you want to know?"

"I want to know what is going on with you. What are you fighting so hard against and why do you run from intimacy?"

"Not asking for much, are you?" I tried to laugh, but in reality, my chest was tight. This was what I needed to talk about, but...

"Let's start slow. One step at a time. What made you move here, besides work?" Nick sat back against the rock, pulling me back with him.

"I was running away from my past, hoping to find peace."

"Did you find it?"

I shook my head. "Not yet." I paused. "I know you need to know things, but I'm not sure I'm ready to talk about it."

I held my breath waiting for the other shoe to drop...I handed him the chance to walk away.

"Don't think you are going to shut me out and forget we had this conversation. I'll give you time you need, but Izzy, you've got to deal with this." Nick sighed softly against my hair.

"I know. I'll get a name from Diane for someone to talk to."

twenty-two

Work was dragging. I couldn't enjoy my day as, in a couple of hours, I would be headed to my first counseling session. Although I knew this was needed, I dreaded it. I had one experience with a counselor and it was not good. I was a master of hiding everything. To dig in and reveal the pain inside, well that was just agony.

The more I tried to throw myself into work, the more distracted I became. Finally, four p.m. rolled around and although I normally would have worked at least another three or four hours, I was toast. My mind was numb with fear of this upcoming event.

"Isabelle?" I turned towards Gayle's office. She was standing in the doorway looking at me with a puzzled looked.

"Yes?"

"Are you okay? I've been calling you."

I was mortified. "Of course. I'm sorry, just my mind was elsewhere." I took a deep breath. "What can I do for you?"

"Was just checking on the Frost book cover."

"I emailed the graphics department this morning on an update. They said we should have it tomorrow."

Gayle nodded and turned to step back inside her office. "If you need to leave, go ahead. You work late all the time. It's okay to leave a little early tonight and have some down time. You've been working hard."

I sighed. "Maybe I will. I hate to, but I really need to clear my head."

"Go ahead. I'll see you tomorrow." With those words, Gayle had disappeared again back into her own work cave. I gathered myself and shut the computer off. I did need a little bit of time to myself. A walk on the beach would help calm the nerves before I went to my counseling session.

I pulled up in front of the office complex, exhaling slowly as I shut my car off. Moment of truth...literally. No more hiding behind the facade of life is good. I glanced at my watch for the hundredth time in the past hour. I was ten minutes early. Perfect timing. I exited my vehicle and made my way to the office.

Diane had given me the name of this counselor, saying, "Mary is the best." Well, that remained to be seen. Chest tightness came over me as I walked in the door and sat down. The waiting room was empty and there was no place to check in. The inner office door was shut. I assumed she was still with someone as I flipped through a magazine. I hadn't waited long when the office door opened and a young woman came walking out.

"You must be Isabelle." She smiled and extended her hand. "Mary Rourke."

"Yes, nice to meet you." I shook her hand and she gestured for me to enter the office. As I walked in, I took in the surroundings. A pair of comfortable wingtip chairs, a love seat and a desk. One was a floor to ceiling bookcase, filled to the brim with books. I walked closer to the book case and scanned the books. Mostly psychology books with some thrillers mixed in.

Mary settled into one of the chairs and waited for me. I glanced at the love seat and then the chair. I sat down in the chair across from her. Crossed my legs and uncrossed them again. She just sat there watching me, not saying anything. My nerves were frazzled.

"This first session is just a get to know you one. No worries. We're not going to dive into anything too deep today." She smiled encouragingly at me.

I nodded. "I'm not usually on edge like this."

"It's understandable. Everyone gets a little nervous going to see the 'shrink'." She laughed as she air quoted the word shrink. I smiled. "Just tell me a little bit about why you are here."

I took a deep breath. "Well, I'm stuck. I guess that's the best way to describe it."

"Stuck with what?" She prompted.

"Life." I laughed. "I can't seem to get past some things that happened in the past and well, it's really starting to impact my life, I guess."

"Okay. Well, tell me about your family of origin."

I was antsy and couldn't sit. I stood and wandered around the room, stopping in front of her window that looked over the local park. "Well, not much to tell. I was an only child. Parents are still married. The usual."

"Was it a good childhood do you think?"

"Well, I wasn't abused." I turned towards her, confused by the question.

She nodded. "There are many aspects that make up

a good childhood. Some people are in perfectly capable homes, no abuse, and yet still don't feel they have had a good childhood." She watched me. I turned back to the window, biting my bottom lip. A good childhood. I didn't even know the meaning of that.

"I honestly don't know. What constitutes a good childhood? I had food on the table, a roof over my head, friends in school." I shrugged and returned to the chair.

"And?"

I shook my head. "And what?"

"Were you happy?"

I couldn't help it, the laughter bubbled up in me. It was comical to think that I had ever been happy in my life. That was why I ran away from the past, wasn't it? She nodded at me, encouraging me to elaborate. "I don't know what happy is." Those simple words slipped out of my mouth without me thinking about it. Soberness hit me. I really didn't. I just stared at Mary, not knowing what else to say.

"Well, there it is. Our starting point."

I sighed as tears rushed my eyes. I blinked and blinked, willing them not to fall. I would not become this emotional wreck. I had held on all these years, I wasn't about to cave now.

"I think some people confuse happiness and contentment. Happiness comes and goes with circumstances. Contentment is what we find inside when we realize that we're okay in every sense of the word – physically, mentally, emotionally. As a child, we don't recognize that happiness comes and goes so it's easier to talk about a happy childhood where if the majority of your memories were good ones, you probably had a happy childhood. However, if your memories are more yearning or internally painful, well, then probably not so happy. That doesn't necessary come from a bad childhood or a traumatic event that happened to you. Sometimes we don't even know what we yearn for." Mary paused.

"I wouldn't say I had a bad childhood, just not a childhood filled with love and laughter. Don't get me wrong. I love my grandparents and are very close with them. Not so close with my parents really." I shrugged.

"No siblings?"

I shook my head no. I felt myself start to relax. This wasn't so bad.

"Tell me about your parents."

"Not much to tell. My dad is a hard-working man, provider. My mother is...well, she was a stay-at-home mom, very critical. I don't really keep in contact with them that often." I bit my bottom lip. "I just stay busy with work here. Doesn't leave much time for phone calls and such."

Mary wrote quietly on her pad of paper and nodded. "What's your earliest memory of feeling disjointed from your family?"

"Disjointed?" I was surprised by the question. It was the perfect description of how I had felt for years. "I think on some level I felt like I never fit it, or least with my parents. I'm very close to my grandparents."

"When did that start?"

"I'm not sure...but I remember being in sixth grade and overhearing a conversation between my parents where my mom was upset about not having her career anymore and was mad that she had given up everything for me." I paused. I hadn't thought of that conversation in years. "Her anger at having a child was so...palpable in the air, I just didn't want to be there anymore."

"Are you sure that was directed at you or was it just frustration on her part at missing her career?" Mary's question was reasonable, yet it struck a chord in me.

"How would any child take that? They hear their mother say they gave up everything for their child and are angry." I stood and started pacing the room.

"I'm not doubting your feelings. Just digging a little deeper."

"I'd rather not talk about that."

Mary watched me. "Did your parents have any siblings?"

"My father didn't. Mom had one sister who died before I was born." I glanced at my watch.

"I think we're out of time today. How about for next week you put together a family tree?"

"I could do that. How far back?" I was curious, and had never thought much about genealogy.

"That's up to you." Mary stood.

I nodded and headed for the door. I was ready to get home. Suddenly I was emotionally exhausted and needed to just to stare out at the ocean and let my mind rest.

twenty-three

My mind was reeling as I took the steps two at a time to my apartment. There in front of the door was Nick bearing a bottle of wine and take out.

"Eaten yet?" He held up the bag of food.

I sighed and shook my head no. "I'm exhausted though."

"I figured, but I also knew you wouldn't eat. So, food, complete silence with a good friend." He flashed me a smile and I couldn't resist.

"Fine. Come on in. But seriously, complete silence."

He gestured zipping his lips and followed me into the apartment. I escaped to the bedroom to get into my comfy clothes -- sweats and my favorite oversized sweatshirt. I sat on the edge of the bed listening to Nick whistling in the kitchen as he pulled out plates and glasses from the cupboards. Although mentally I didn't want to deal with anything, I was comforted by the fact he was there for me. He was a good man, and I although I cared for him, my heart still ached for Jack and I knew it was unfair to Nick to feel that way.

I made my way out of the bedroom and saw Nick carrying the plates to the deck. Wine was already poured and on the table outside. I wandered out and sank into a chair. Taking a long sip of wine, I closed my eyes and listened to the waves. Stress washed away from me with every lap of the waves on the beach. This was my happy place.

I opened my eyes and glanced at Nick. He was looking out to the ocean, drinking his wine. "Thank you."

He put a finger to his lips. "Shhhh."

I smiled, realizing I was starving and dug into dinner with gusto. We ate in silence and after the food was done, and Nick had cleared the plates, we sat enjoying another glass of wine. "Are you going to ask me about today?"

"Nope."

"Really?"

He shrugged. "If you want to share, you will. I'm not going to pry. I'm here simply for moral support."

I finished my glass of wine and set down the glass. I rose and went to the railing, looking out to the ocean. "I really appreciate it, the food, wine, company without questions. But it wasn't too bad. I have a feeling it's going to get worse though."

"Well, small steps."

"True." I turned and leaned against the railing, watching Nick. "I need your help."

"With what?" He raised an eyebrow at me.

"I'm supposed to do a genealogy for next week. I hate that kind of stuff."

"Ahhh…you want to cheat already on your homework." Nick finished his wine and set down his glass.

"It's not really cheating." I shrugged. "Never mind."

Nick laughed. "Don't get cranky. I didn't say I wouldn't help."

I stuck my tongue out at him. "I'm not cranky."

He reached for my hand and pulled me closer to him. "How hard can it be?"

I laid my hand on his chest and felt his heart beating. I paused as I allowed my fingers to hear his heart. Why did someone else's heartbeat have such an impact on me? This was the first heartbeat I had listened to since Jack's. Jack. I sighed and looked up into his blue eyes. I felt the physical pain of being torn between my past and my present. I closed my eyes when I felt him cover my hand on his chest with his. The warmth of his hand over mine pulled at me.

"Izzy?" His voice was soft and I leaned closer as I opened my eyes. His face was so close to mine. My eyes went to his lips, so close to mine, and I just wanted to kiss them. Instead I drew my eyes up to his.

"Yeah?"

I could see the torment in his eyes. "When do you want to start?"

"Start?" My mind had gone blank.

"Your family tree."

I stepped back. "Anytime, tomorrow. I'm too tired tonight to think about that." I had moved back just a little, but Nick was still holding my hand on his chest and his other hand was on my hip. He oozed sexiness and I wanted him, but I wanted the sex, not the intimacy. I just couldn't do it, not right now. I couldn't give him what he wanted and he knew it as he moved his hand off mine and stepped back himself. The moment passed and although not a word was said, Nick picked up the glasses and headed inside to put them in the kitchen.

Meeting me at the door to the apartment. He turned. "Text me when you want my help. I'll let you get some rest."

"Nick...thank you."

He pulled me into a hug. "You know I'm here for you." He kissed me briefly on the cheek and was out the door before I could respond.

I curled up on the couch and replayed the counseling session through my mind. I hadn't had a bad childhood, but it wasn't full of happiness and contentment like Mary talked about. I thought back to the conversation I had overhead between my parents. Was it possible that the anger wasn't really directed at me, my mother's only daughter? Or was she really so angry at me for coming into her life so she had to give up her career? I had no idea. It truly was the only time I ever had heard my mother talk about having a career. There is one thing for sure, my childhood was not simple like most kids had. It was complicated and apparently full of secrets -- both on my part and on the part of my parents.

twenty-four

The next couple of days flew by at work. I was swamped with dealing with cover art and new projects passing through my desk. Gayle and I put in long hours, and for that I was thankful as my mind stayed focused on my work. Life's challenges stayed in the shadows and at night I would go home only to fall into bed exhausted from work, sleep and start the next day over again.

Friday came too quickly and as I glanced at my watch, realizing it was late and I was the only one still in the office. Gayle had cut out at six, stating she was calling it an early night. It was now eight p.m. I made sure a new manuscript that had come in was in my inbox so I could read it this weekend at home, packed up my stuff and decided eight was late enough at the office. My stomach rumbled in protest at the fact that I hadn't eaten all day and suddenly I was very aware of how hungry I was.

I dumped my bag with my computer off at my apartment and started across the street to the beach. I was still in a skirt from work, but I kicked off my heels and allowed my bare feet to sink into the sand. The warmth of the sun from the day had faded and the sand had cooled off. I faced the ocean and closed my eyes, allowing the sound of the waves to soothe my unsettled soul. Conflicted. It was something I admired in characters in the manuscripts I read. I loved a conflicted character and yet here I was the poster child for a conflicted soul.

I inhaled the salt air, opened my eyes and headed down the beach towards the best food shack around. Some comfort food was just what I needed tonight. I still needed to do my homework of putting my family tree together, but I had hesitated to text Nick for his help. When he was around, I just wanted him physically, although his friendship and moral support were great to have to. But those blue eyes…damn those blue eyes were such a turn on. I entered the shack and placed my usual order for fried shrimp and French fries. The carbs I would have to walk off tomorrow, but tonight I just wanted that fried food that for some reason brought a sense of comfort to me.

I sat in a corner table waiting for the food, scrolling through various social media accounts on my phone. I looked up when I heard that familiar deep voice ordering. Nick. Of course, it would be. This was his favorite spot too. Hadn't we come here on our first date? How many dates had we actually had? It was a blur. I immediately turned back to my phone, hoping I could just blend in with the wall behind me.

"May I join you?" I glanced up to see his smile, although it didn't quite reach his eyes.

"Of course." I put my phone aside.

"I'm taking it you decided against my help with your family tree."

I shook my head. "No, I've just haven't gotten home from work before nine any night this week…until tonight."

"Yeah, and eight is so much earlier." He laughed. "Look, Izzy, tell me if I'm pushing too much."

I sighed. "No, you're not. I just…I just am unsure how to navigate this between us now."

"Now?"

"You know what I mean. Sex is easier. But now, friendship, I don't do any type of relationship well whether it is friendship or more."

"So you've said before." Nick glanced up as the waitress brought my food. He waited until she was gone before he continued. "Or maybe you just don't want to put in the effort."

I salted my fries. "How can you say that?"

We both fell silent as the waitress brought Nick's food. I picked at my shrimp, nibbling it, watching him. "Maybe I can say it because of your actions."

I pushed my food away, suddenly not hungry. "My actions? You were the one that laid down the law on what the boundaries were. I could only agree or you were gone."

"Is that how you see it? Eat, Izzy. I guarantee you haven't eaten all day." Nick gestured to my food.

"You're infuriating." I pulled the food closer and started eating. I was hungry, but damn it I wouldn't let him know that. He acted like he knew me, but the truth of the matter was he could see right through me.

We ate in silence. My phone chirped at an incoming text. I picked it up and read:

How about that family tree?

I laughed out loud. "Really? You are going to text me from across the table?"

"I didn't want to interrupt your eating." He smirked at me.

I stuck my tongue out at him. "Fine, I still need your help. I don't even know where to start with it."

"It's not rocket science, Izzy. Start with you and go back." Nick stood and held his hand out to me.

As we left the shack and started walking down the beach, I slipped off my heels again. I was distracted by the thought of the family tree. "It just seems odd to me."

"What does?" Nick glanced at me.

"Why would she want me to do a family tree? I mean…what does it matter?"

"I don't know. Maybe it was something you said that she thought it would be a good exercise for you."

"Ugh. I don't want to." I kicked at the sand.

"I think there's bigger question. Why don't you want to do this?"

"What are you my shrink now?" I bit my bottom lip. That came out harsh, but I was tired and maybe just a little afraid of why I always felt so out of place in my own family.

Nick just laughed. "I thought we established I'm here just as a friend."

I stopped and turned towards him. "What if that isn't what I want?" I tilted my head and watched him.

He smiled that smile that made me weak in the knees. "What is it you want, Izzy?"

What I wanted was for him to step closer to me, to lean in and kiss me like he cared, to take me back to my apartment and just let me forget all that I was facing. But no, instead he stood just out of reach watching me, waiting for my answer.

"I want to hide my head in the sand and not deal with any of this. I want…" I wanted to say *you*, but I couldn't say it. I couldn't be that vulnerable to him.

"Isn't that how we got to this point? You not dealing with any of it and just hiding behind sex." He reached for my hand and started walking again. "Don't get me wrong, Izzy, it was great sex, but I want more from you and you're not ready for that."

I concentrated on the warmth of his hand, fingers intertwined with mine. "I know." The words were a whisper and I'm not even sure he heard them.

"Tell me about your family, Izzy."

"Nothing to tell really." He squeezed my hand to admonish me. "Fine. It was just me, no siblings. I was close to my grandparents on my mother's side. Never knew my father's parents." I shook my head. "I mean that's it. That was the extent of my family."

"No siblings for your parents?"

"My mother had a sister who died before I was born. I never knew her. Dad didn't have any." We jogged across the road to my apartment building. "I don't get it. What am I missing, Nick? There is no other family."

"I don't know." We were silent as we went up the stairs and into my place. I threw my heels down by the door and walked over to the couch. I curled my legs under me and pulled a pillow onto my lap. Nick sat down next to me. "Don't overthink it. Maybe it's just her way of getting you to open up a bit."

"Maybe. But it feels like something else…I don't know what." I sighed. Maybe I was overthinking it. I leaned my head on Nick's shoulder.

twenty-five

Nick stayed and we talked well into the early morning. I fell asleep on him, yet he made no effort to go home. I opened my eyes to the sun shining through the sliding door to the balcony. My head was against Nick's chest. I listened to his heart beat as his chest rose and fell with every breath.

I caught my breath, closed my eyes and listened, concentrating on the steadiness of it. Steadiness. That was Nick to a tee. He didn't waver in his support, regardless of how neurotic I had become. I rose slowly not to wake him and wandered into the kitchen. I started the coffee before heading to the bedroom to shower and change. When I came out, Nick was out on the balcony, his back to the apartment.

I fixed two mugs of coffee and joined him. Handing him one of the mugs, I scanned his face for something that would give away what he was thinking. He showed no emotion. "Thanks" was the only thing he said before he turned back to the ocean.

"Nick…" I didn't know what to say. I looked at the ocean and could feel his gaze upon me. I glanced at him and shrugged.

He let out a soft sigh and drained his coffee. "I'm going to head home." He gave me a kiss on the cheek and went into the apartment.

I followed him into the kitchen. "What is going on?"

"You tell me. You can't tell me what you want, you hold me at arm's length. Damn it, Izzy, I'm here and it's like you don't even see me." He threw his hands up in frustration.

"That's not true, Nick." My voice was soft and I looked down at my coffee. I saw his fingers wrap around my mug and take it from my hands. Raising my eyes to meet his, he pulled me closer and held me close. I softened my rigid stance and for the first time allowed myself to totally relax against him. My hands balled his t-shirt into my fist as I held him close to me. He exuded strength and that I strength I couldn't soak in fast enough or even enough of it to keep me going. "Let's talk."

I straightened and pulled back from him. He nodded. Once settled onto the couch, me with my legs pulled up under me, facing him. He sat at the other end of the couch just out of reach. "Don't say anything. Just let me get this out while I have the nerve."

He nodded. I took a deep breath and closed my eyes for a moment. When I opened them he was just sitting there, watching me, waiting. "Nick, there are things I have never talked about. Didn't tell people I should have and hurt them in the process because I didn't know how…how to handle things." I sighed. I swallowed hard, my throat dry, restricting on me reminding me of that night…that night. He waited.

"When I was eighteen, I overdosed. Well, I…I tried to kill myself." He leaned toward me and I raised my hand to hold him off. "No, no pity. Just listen."

He sat back, but I could tell by the look of his face he wasn't happy about me keeping my distance. "I obviously failed. One more life failure and yes, that is how I felt at the time. I couldn't even off myself and get it right."

"Izzy." His voice was laced with shock.

I shook my head. "After I quit college, my parents didn't want me to go back. Told everyone I didn't know what I wanted to do with my life, but the reality was we just never talked about 'the incident'. I have spent the last seven years pretending it didn't happen, and pretending that I was whole when I'm obviously not." I choked back the tears that threatened to spill. I rubbed my throat. The constriction was a reminder of that night, when I swallowed pill after pill. "I thought I found happiness, but was told I had no right to be happy so instead…"

"The reason you hide behind sex and no emotions." Nick broke in. There was no criticism, just fact.

I nodded. "I don't know how to get past this, or past…" I couldn't bring myself to tell him about Jack and how my heart still belonged to Jack regardless of the years that had gone by or how it ended. I truly believed in life that you could fall in love many times over the course of your life, but there was only one true love for each of us. Whether we came together and the timing was wrong or if, like me, I walked away from the best thing I ever had in my life and forced us to part.

"Who told you that you had no right to be happy?"

Nick scooted across the couch until my knees touched him. "Who would do that to you? You were just eighteen."

I looked at him. Tears clung to my eyelashes, on the brink of spilling. "Does it matter?"

"Maybe it does for you to heal."

I closed my eyes and a solitary tear made its way down my cheek. I felt Nick's warm finger brush it away. His finger trailed down my jaw, caressing me. I opened my eyes as he removed his hand.

"You pushed me to deal with this. And I'm not saying that is bad, I know I should, but it's killing me to face this."

"You haven't talked about this since it happened?"

"No. It was never spoken of again after they came to the hospital to pick me up." I stretched my legs over Nick's and hugged a pillow close.

He rubbed my legs. "Another cup of coffee?"

"You're staying?" I questioned as I nodded yes to the coffee.

"I'm not leaving. We're not really done talking, are we?"

I shook my head no and lifted my legs for him to go get more coffee. As Nick left the living room, I watched him, yet my mind was on Jack. Would Jack have reacted the same way if I had told him all those years ago? Would he have stayed by myself? I sighed. Life would have been so different. What ifs. I could lose myself in playing the what if game, and yet it was futile to even think about it.

Once Nick was resituated on the couch and we were drinking out coffee, Nick turned to me. "Have you dated anyone since then? I mean really date."

I felt my eyes widen and I tried to keep my face neutral. I nodded briefly. "Just once."

"Izzy, he's the one who broke your heart?"

"No." I was quick with the answer and took a deep breath. "Quite the opposite. I broke my own heart. I forced him to walk away from us because I believed I couldn't be happy even though he made me happy. He was so hurt." I couldn't stem the tears as they started to flow. Seven years of never mentioning Jack, crying only in solitude with no one ever knowing how much pain I was in.

"You never told him about the suicide attempt?" Nick's voice spoke of shock and unbelief.

"We were young. I didn't know how to handle it." I brushed my tears aside. "And before you ask, yes, I loved him. I was young, but I knew that I loved him with all my heart. His heartbeat was mine. I know that sounds ridiculous, but…"

"Your one true love. I get it. I know we all have one true love. That doesn't mean you don't get to love again, Izzy." Nick's eyes searched mine. The blue deepened with concern.

I could tell he had more questions, but I wasn't ready to answer them…or even face the enormity of the truth at this point. "Enough for right now. I can't talk about this anymore." I was relieved when Nick nodded and finished his coffee.

"Movie?"

"What?"

He grinned at me. "Let's watch a comedy and lounge today. I think after the hours you've been working, you deserve at least a morning to just relax."

twenty-six

The weekend flew by. Nick and I spent Saturday binge watching movies and ordering in Chinese food. I felt a burden lift off my shoulders after we had talked. He may not know everything, but he had a glimpse into me and what made me tick. He seemed content with that. He had stayed Saturday night just holding me all night as we laid in bed. There had been nothing sexual about it, but the safety of his arms gave me a bit of confidence that talking about the past would be okay.

I rose Monday early. I had tossed and turned most of the night Sunday night and had actually missed Nick not being there. Filling my travel mug with coffee, I headed out to the office two hours earlier than usual. I arrived at six a.m., and loved the quietness. The phones were silent, printers, no tapping of keyboards. Just pure silence, unintrusive silence.

By the time Gayle came walking through the door at 7:30, I had already caught up on all my emails and put the finishing touches on the manuscript I was editing.

"You don't usually beat me," Gayle announced, surprised to see me.

"Couldn't sleep." I grinned at her. "You must be rubbing off on me."

"I'm not sure if that is a good or a bad thing." She laughed as she waltzed into her office. "Cover art meeting at eight."

"Way ahead of you. Already looked at the digital mock ups. I don't think it will take long to give the final go ahead in the meeting. You'll see there really is only one choice." I called into her office from my desk.

She came to the doorway. "What has gotten into you? Gunning for my job?"

"Nope, I don't want your job. I'm content right here for now."

The day flew by with meetings. Cover art was chosen for the next release. I had sent off my edits to a new author I was working with and was in the process of going through submissions that had come through my email box when Gayle came to my desk. "You realize it's six already. I think a twelve-hour day is long enough, really, especially with all that you did today."

I glanced up. "I'm just looking over submissions."

"Not tonight. Take the night off, seriously. You work harder than anyone I know in this office. When was the last time you actually left the office before eight or nine?"

"Honestly, I don't know. I'm not sure I'll know what to do with myself." I knew Gayle was serious though so I packed up myself. "Okay, I'm headed home."

"And don't read submissions tonight," Gayle called

behind me. I threw my hand up to acknowledge her and waved as I left our office.

I headed home, completely at a loss at what I should be doing at this time of night. A definite rarity for me. I dropped my bag off at the apartment and changed quickly into yoga pants and a t-shirt. I approached the beach and headed down to the water, flip-flops in hand. I walked slowly through the small waves lapping at my ankles towards the rocky cove where I had met Nick.

The weekend had been nice, but the reality of it was Nick and I were no closer, or further apart for that matter, after talking. I did feel lighter not carrying the silence of the suicide attempt. I thought back to that night in my dorm room. Life had seemed so dismal, no future. If only I had known at that point that I was going to meet Jack, or be living in Virginia. Although working in the publishing world had never crossed my mind at that age.

Self-reflection was a dangerous path for me. I knew this and yet I continued to rehash over and over the events and how I might have been able to change things. I often wondered what Jack was doing. I hoped he had found happiness. He deserved it after all.

In true Isabelle form, I tried to run through every scenario possible for my next counseling session. Although impossible to figure out what she would ask, I knew I needed to be open, and yet in reality I would be guarded. I was supposed to be there tomorrow evening. Sighing, I went through my family tree one more time, although I never pursued going further than my grandparents on my mother's side. I never knew the grandparents on my father's side and it didn't seem to matter to me.

I had come to the end of the beach. I glanced at the rock cove and turned away. Home. Maybe a little bit of

TV and a glass of wine would relax me. Maybe even an early night to bed and hopefully a full night's sleep without dreams intruding.

My phone vibrated as a text came in. *Home yet?* It was Nick.

I typed a quick reply. *Yup, but walking on the beach. What's up?*

Want some company?

Yes. I'll be home in 5.

I picked up the pace and headed home. I needed Nick, not just as a friend…he had to see that. Or tonight, maybe at least he would give up this nonsense of no sex and at least give us both some relief.

I hadn't been home for two minutes before Nick was knocking. I flung open the door and gestured for him to enter. He pushed the door shut behind him and pulled me into a hug. I ran my hands up his back. He pulled me closer and his hands ran slowly down my hips, grabbing my butt, grinding against me. Oh, this man was missing me as much as I was him.

I pulled back my head to look at him and he groaned as his lips captured mine. I stroked his tongue with mine, sucking gently. He backed me against the wall, grabbing my hands and raising them above my head. He pulled back, his eyes locked on mine. "Izzy, I wasn't going to do this. You are so damn irresistible." His mouth locked with mine again as he pinned me to the wall.

I moaned softly against him. His mouth moved from my lips down my jawline, stopping at the base of my neck. His feathery kisses brought goosebumps to my skin as I turned my neck to give him more access. He straightened and stepped back,

"Nick." The single word was barely a whisper and somewhere between an admonishment and a question.

"Izzy, I don't want to further complicate things."

I reached out to him and pulled him close. "It's not a complication. It's what we both want." I nuzzled my face into his neck as I closed my eyes.

"Yes, I do want you. Damn it, I'm so hard right now and all I can think about is laying you down on that bed in there and bringing you to the point where you forget everything and everyone but me."

I nodded. The *everyone* was what was bothering him. My memories of Jack, although a nameless love to Nick. "He's not here, Nick. This is just you and me." I looked at him and waited a second before I grabbed his hand and had him follow me into the bedroom. I turned as I entered the bedroom, letting go of his hand. I tugged him closer by the end of his t-shirt and as he took a step closer, I pulled the t-shirt up and over his head. I dropped it and ran my hands up his biceps, onto his shoulders and down his chest, stopping at the top of his jeans.

I smiled at him as I undid the button of his jeans, and slowly unzipped them. My hands moved to hips just inside his jeans and stopped. My thumbs made small circles on his inner hips. He stood there, waiting. I could see his jaw clench as he tried to control himself and stay still. I moved my hand to the elastic of his boxers and slid my fingers under the waist band, sliding them along his skin.

Nick groaned and grabbed my hands, pushing me backwards until the back of my knees hit the bed. He yanked my t-shirt off and unhooked my bra in a single move. I was naked from the waist up. He pulled the same seductive move, although instead of my thighs, his thumbs made circles around my nipples, making them hard pebbles, aching for his mouth to close over them. I closed my eyes and moaned softly, my hands grabbing on to the edge of his jeans so I would fall backwards.

I heard a small chuckle and my eyes flew open. Nick was watching me. His hands had stilled. I shook my head at him, silently begging him not to stop. He nipped me softly at the neck, just enough to send an electric shock through me. I couldn't wait. My hands slid down and stroked the length of him. He allowed it for a what seemed like only seconds before he pushed me backwards on to the bed. He pulled my clothing on my lower half off in one swift move, shedding his own just as quickly.

As he stood over me and I looked up at him, I knew this moment would be a pivotal moment in our relationship. He needed to claim me, erase the memories he knew I was carrying. Without a thought, I nodded and reached for him. He entered me in one sudden motion. I cried out, not in pain, but the sheer awareness of the message he was sending. I bit his shoulder as he thrust harder and faster in me. The waves of ecstasy engulfing me sending me over the edge. He cried out my name as he shuddered in release.

As we crawled under the covers once we had recovered, Nick turned towards me. I snuggled up to him, catching him off guard. "Izzy, I'm sorry."

"For what? You better not be sorry for what just happened." I was furious at the apology.

"I wasn't gentle."

I smiled. "You were exactly what I needed in that moment. You were mine and I yours. Don't ever apologize to me for that."

He kissed the top of my forehead and pulled me close. We laid in silence, enjoying the closeness, physical and emotional that had finally come into play.

twenty-seven

Morning brought with it a feeling of laziness. Never in my life had I wanted to just lay in bed pass when my alarm went off than I did today. In fact, I was always up before the alarm went off and here I was curled up in Nick's arms wishing that damn beeping would stop. Nick reached out and hit the off button.

"Morning." He kissed me and stood. I watched him stretch as he walked to the bathroom. I grinned. Who would have thought I would actually enjoy having a naked man waking up next to me instead of cringing? I couldn't help but laugh.

I glanced at the clock. Six a.m. I needed to be to work in an hour if I was going to leave early for counseling. I jumped out of bed and walked into the bathroom. Nick was just starting the shower. "Make it fast, buddy. I've got to get to work."

He gestured towards the steaming water. "Join me. I promise to behave."

"I make no such promises." I gave him a swat on his ass as I moved into the water.

"Feisty this morning. This is quite a change from the last time when you couldn't wait for me to leave."

I ignored the comment as I shampooed and rinsed, hogging the hot water the best I could before I finally relented to him getting under the spray as I stepped out. I was dressed in an A-line skirt and blouse by the time he came out of the bathroom. I made up the bed and whistled at him when he dropped his towel to get dressed. He gave me a look that made me realize if I wanted to get to work on time, I needed to go make the coffee, out of sight of Nick.

I pulled out my second travel mug and fixed both of them. By the time Nick arrived in the kitchen, coffee was ready to go and so was I. "Wow, here's your coffee, there's the door." Nick joked.

"You know I have to get to work early today. I have to leave in time to go to my next counseling session."

He nodded. "You ready for it?"

"I think so. I think it helped a little bit to tell you about…anyway, I think maybe I can talk about it with her."

"About…say it, Izzy. It's okay. It is a part of your life. Don't be ashamed of it anymore." Nick reached for my hand.

"The suicide attempt." I stuck my tongue out at him. "It's hard to get past it after years of never mentioning it."

He gave me a lingering kiss before we parted, each headed off to start the day. Nick would need to run home and grab some clean clothes. Maybe we should think ahead of that next time. Work flew by. I was caught up on most things and was able to pick up a new manuscript from the submission pile to start reading. The alarm on my phone alerted me to when it was time to leave.

My stomach clenched in apprehension as I approached Mary's office. As usual her inside office door was shut so I settled myself into a chair in the waiting room. Within minutes, she opened the door.

"Come on in, Isabelle."

"Hi." I wandered in and immediately went to the windows. Peering out past the park, to the distant ocean, I allowed the mesmerizing motion of the waves hitting the beach calm me.

"Okay. Let's start with the family tree." Wow. She didn't hold back.

"I'm not sure why you wanted me to do this."

Mary looked up from her notebook and tilted her head at me. "Did you do the family tree?"

"In my head. There isn't much. I don't have a lot of family."

She nodded. "Sit down, Isabelle." She waited while I moved to the couch and sat. "The reason for the family tree isn't just about the people you already know. It's about going deeper and discovering family you didn't know you had. You said you felt a disconnect from your family of origin. Well, what if you have an ancestor further back in your line that was an author. Maybe that is the reason you had a desire to get into the publishing field. Do you see my point? This isn't about your family of origin. Of course, you know them."

I nodded. "I never thought of it that way."

"Good. You can finish that for next week. Let's move on." Mary was all business today and I immediately put my guard up. "What do you want to talk about today?"

"I don't know." I shrugged.

Mary smiled. "Well, we're not going to help you get to where you want to be if we don't dive into it."

I stood and sat back down. I needed to wander, to see the ocean. I stood again and wandered back to the window.

"What is it about being over there?" Mary asked.

"I can see the ocean. The ocean is calming to me. I love hearing the waves lap the beach, or crash against the rocks. I can spend hours listening to it, watching it. It's my happy place."

"Why do you need a happy place down here? I thought you left New Hampshire to find happiness." Mary prodded.

I sighed. "What I found out is that you can't outrun your past."

"What are you trying to outrun?" Mary was patient, but I could picture her almost make the gesture of pumping water from a well to pull the information from me.

I turned and leaned against the window sill. "My past." I smiled when she raised an eyebrow at me. "I know, you want more than that." I took a deep breath. "A suicide attempt, a lost love, a family that acted like they hated me."

Mary stopped writing and locked eyes with me. "Whoa. That's a lot to try and outrun." She stood and walked over to me, leaning against the window sill next to me. "Let's start a little slower."

I cut her off. "I was eighteen. I overdosed."

"The question isn't how you did it, but why." Mary's voice was soft.

"I didn't see a future. I was in the dark place and felt so unloved, and all I wanted was someone to love me for me." The words rushed out of me. I took a breath. "Why is it so hard to find someone to love you?" Anguish shook through me.

"Have you never been in love, Isabelle?" Mary moved back to her chair and picked up her pen and paper again.

"I've been in love, but I couldn't...we didn't..." The tears rolled down my cheek for the second time in a week at the thought of how I had hurt Jack.

"First of all, you're not going to heal overnight. Some wounds take longer and especially ones that you have ignored for years."

I nodded. "Seven years I haven't talked about this. It was never talked about after the attempt. My parents ignored it, acted like it never happened."

"You have to realize that is their issue, not yours. I know that isn't what you needed at the time, but right now in this very moment, you are stepping over the threshold between pain and healing. You need to take the step for yourself, not hold back based on others' actions."

"They were my parents. How could they act like they didn't care about me at all? Like it never happened? It wasn't something stupid like I shoplifted something...I tried to kill myself." I clenched my hands together to stop the trembling.

"Isabelle." Mary's voice broke through the haze of my thoughts. "You have people in your life right now, don't you, that love you? That care what happens to you?"

"Yes. That's why I'm here. Nick wanted me to face this stuff because I hold myself aloft from relationships and I just can't allow that kind of intimacy in my life. I won't be hurt, or hurt someone else again."

Mary nodded. "Let's start with you not hurting you."

"What do you mean? I'm not suicidal anymore. I would never do that now."

"That's not what I meant. Shutting yourself off emotionally from others hurts you. You lose out on some of the greatest moments shared with another being by closing yourself off." Mary paused. She sighed. "My guess is the phrase you said a minute ago of 'hurt someone else again' is something that you carry with you. Tell me about that."

I shook my head. "No. Not now."

Mary glanced at her watch. "Fair enough. Maybe we should stop for today. I think you shared quite a bit, heavy stuff today, and probably need to process it. Let's meet again next week and seriously, Isabelle, do the family tree. I think it might help you."

I nodded. "Thanks. I will work on it."

I left Mary's office drained and feeling off kilter. The buoyance I felt this morning was gone and in its place was an anchor around my neck. I just wanted to curl up in bed and cry myself to sleep. As I sat in my car, I checked my phone and found a text from Nick. *Thinking of you. We'll talk tomorrow. If you need me sooner, call.*

I sent a quick text back. *Thanks. Tomorrow's good. I'm tired and am going to head to bed early.*

I pulled into the parking lot of my apartment and sat there. Jack, why did it have to be this way. You should be here with me, enjoying the ocean. The thought wasn't an unusual one to run through my head and I had a feeling before this counseling gig was over, Jack was going to be in my head a lot as I struggled to work through the past. The day I met Jack was the moment I realized I wanted to live. Little did I know back then that our paths would be obstacle-riddled and at times seemingly impossible to get through.

Tomorrow was another day. Back to work and I would use my energy to refocus on new submissions hoping to find that next new bestseller.

twenty-eight

Although I had been drained from my session with Mary, sleep had eluded me. I crawled out of bed at five a.m. fed up with the tossing and turning. As I waited for my morning jolt to brew, I stood at the balcony doors watching the waves. It's funny how instinctively I moved to Virginia to be close to this--the ocean, beautiful and majestic.

The beeping of the coffee pot brought me to the present. I poured my coffee and closed my eyes as I inhaled the aroma before taking that first magical sip. The ritual of inhaling the scent of the coffee before taking a sip was one I indulged in forever. It gave that first sip a such fuller flavor. It was a routine that I relied on to keep me grounded in the present. I sat down at the kitchen table and opened my laptop.

Genealogy. I had no idea even where to start. I had heard of web sites that talked about tracing ancestors. I did a Google search and came up with one that looked good. I clicked on it and started reading how it worked.

Oh, there was so much more to this than I had thought. I had a notebook handy, although once registered on the site it apparently created a little tree and you could save it there.

I added myself onto the tree. Then my parents. A little pop up appeared stating there was information on my parents. I clicked on it and found their date of marriage. No children were listed. I shrugged. I had no idea if that was normal or not. It listed both sets of parents and a button to click on to add them to the tree. After adding them to the tree, more pop ups appeared to add their parents and their parents. As I perused the site, I was seeing that my grandparents had children listed on their informational page that popped up. I went back again to my parents. No children listed.

I went back to my maternal grandmother's page. Both my mother, Marie, and her sister, Sarah, were listed as children. I clicked to add Sarah to the family tree. Her informational page popped up and it listed her date of birth. Under that was a notation of one child, name unknown. I had a cousin? I wracked my brain to try and remember if my parents had ever mentioned Aunt Sarah having children. They had said she died before I was born. Nothing else. As per the norm in the family, it wasn't talked about.

I finished my cup of coffee and went to pour myself a second. I grabbed my cell phone and sent a quick text. *Ok, working on the family tree. Weird stuff.*

I had no sooner sat back down before my phone was vibrating. *Weird good or bad?*

I laughed. Leave it to Nick. *I'm not sure. Need your help tonight.*

I'll be there and will bring dinner. Don't come home too late from work. Eat at 7?

That works. I sat back and stared at the computer. I could always call Gram. I needed to talk to her anyway. It had been too long.

I shut the computer and picked up my coffee mug. Settling on the couch to look out the window, I sipped my coffee. It was too early to call Gram, but I would call her at lunch today from work.

I lazed around home as much as I could before it was driving me nuts and still ended up at work an hour earlier than normal. I went through emails, which there always seemed to be an overabundance of before hitting the submission pile again. I sent off an email to my author to see where she was with edits. Her deadline was today and I hadn't heard from her. She hadn't communicated an issue with meeting the deadline. I prayed she would get them to me today so I could start on them while still at work. I wanted to devote tonight to working with Nick on the family tree. I couldn't help but grin at the change in my attitude. Just a few weeks ago, nothing would have gotten in the way of me working well into the night even at home.

As luck would have it, I spent the rest of the day working side by side with Gayle on a new project she was undertaking with the marketing department for a veteran author. She had proved herself in her writing and sales, enough that the company was willing to take on a part of her marketing expenses. As Gayle and I worked through different options for advertising and created a budget, all thoughts of family were gone.

I even worked through lunch and forgot about calling Gram. As my phone vibrated, I glanced down and saw that it was 6:30 pm. *Eating at 7.*

Leave it to Nick to think I needed a reminder. Okay, well, I did, but that was beside the point. *On my way.*

There was something comforting about someone looking after me. A feeling of contentment passed over me along with excitement to actually go home to someone. Just as I expected, Nick was outside my door waiting for me when I arrived. I should really give him a key crossed my mind and I paused. No way. That was not something I would be doing.

I went to change as Nick headed to the kitchen. I didn't know what he had brought, but it smelled good and my stomach signaled that it had once again been ignored all day. Eating really wasn't something I thought of when I was working, unless I got a text from Nick reminding me to eat. I chuckled to myself.

Nick had set up dinner at the table. Steak tip salads. He was patiently waiting for me. I was once again struck by this man sitting at my table just waiting for me, waiting for me to get home from work, waiting for me to finish what I was doing without ever once complaining. I sighed inwardly. That wouldn't last. It never did. Maybe there was no such thing as unconditional love.

We ate dinner pretty much in silence, other than the occasional conversation about our days. I had forgotten to call my grandmother. "Before we get started on the family tree, I need to call Gram."

Nick nodded. I still hadn't filled him in on the fact that there were no kids listed for my parents on the ancestry web site. I was hoping that Gram would provide answers. "Call her and I'll clean up."

I nodded and grabbed my phone. Dialing my grandparents, I settled onto the couch while I waited for an answer.

"Hello."

"Hi, Gram."

"Izzy. How are you? Papa and I were just saying we hadn't heard from you."

"I know, Gram. I'm sorry. Work has been busy, and I know that's not an excuse. I miss you guys."

"We miss you too. But you're living your life and that is what you should be doing. Papa and I do our thing. You know Papa, braiding rugs in the evening with that ole big band music going. Every time Louis Armstrong comes on he wonders how you're doing."

I wiped a tear away. "I miss those evenings, sitting with you guys."

"You okay, honey?"

"Yeah, Gram…kind of. I started going to a counselor to finally deal with the suicide attempt." There was a pause and I heard the second line pick up. "Hi, Papa."

"My Izzy. Tell us what's going on." Leave it to my papa and gram to just let me talk to them. There was never any judgement from them, just love and even all these miles away, I could feel their love coming through the phone.

"I started counseling, Papa. You guys know the suicide attempt was never talked about. For seven years, no one has mentioned it and I just can't get past it."

"I never understood why we were told not to talk about it. It didn't seem right to me." Gram spoke.

"We may not have agreed with it, but it was Marie's wishes. We did what we thought was right at the time in agreeing to it." Papa reprimanded Gram gently.

"Why did Mom not want to talk about it? Was I that big of a disappointment to her?"

"It's more complicated than that, Izzy. You know nothing is ever clear cut. There is always complications and reasons for why people do what they do. Your mother, well, she had a hard time dealing with Sarah's death. She would never talk about it. And she was so angry about it." This was the first I had heard anyone mention my Aunt Sarah and Gram just spoke like Mom was the only one that never spoke of it.

"You never mention Aunt Sarah, Gram."

"No, not around you because it made your mother upset. Papa and I remember Sarah all the time and reminisce about what a free spirit she was. You are so much like her. You have spunk just like her."

Papa cut in. "Every day growing up you have reminded us of her. It helped us keep her with us, Izzy."

"What happened to her? How did she die?" The silence that followed my questions was deafening. I broke the silence. "I've been doing a family tree. The web site I have been using said she had a child."

Gram sighed. "You really should be talking to your parents about this, Izzy."

"Why? What do Mom and Dad have to do with Aunt Sarah having a baby? Did the baby die?"

"Oh, Izzy. No, the baby didn't die." Papa spoke. "But I really think you need to call your mother and ask her about this."

I sat there staring into space. What was going on? "How did Aunt Sarah die?" I wasn't letting this go. I needed an answer.

"She lost too much blood. She had a blood disorder and was always pushing the envelope on things that she shouldn't be doing…things that were risky for her. She had no fear. I have never seen someone so fearless. She had some other medical issues, and well, there was a complication from the childbirth…she just couldn't recover and died a few days after the baby came." Gram's voice cracked with emotion.

"What other medical issues?"

I could hear Papa murmuring to Gram, but couldn't make out the words. Gram came back on the phone. "Izzy, I just can't talk about this right now. Know that I love you dearly."

With a click my grandmother had hung up the phone. I started to hang up and then Papa spoke. "Izzy, I'm only going to say this once and you have to respect the fact that you need to talk to your mother about this. Gram and I can't answer your questions, no matter how much we want to. We both love you so much."

"What is it, Papa?"

"Sarah wasn't supposed to have children, it was too much of a risk for her with her medical issues, but she wanted a child so badly."

"What happened to the baby?" I whispered. My gut clenched and I held my breath waiting for the answer.

"No more questions, Izzy. I love you. I need to go check on your grandmother. Call us when you can." Before I could respond, Papa was gone and I was sitting there holding the phone, dread filling my soul.

I looked up to see Nick standing in the kitchen doorway. I don't know much he heard, but from the look of his face he had heard enough. I just shook my head. I couldn't feel my hands and feet. Numbness crept over me leaving me paralyzed with fear of what I would find out if I went down this path. "I can't do it." The words came out of nowhere. My family was a black hole and God only knows what secrets were within that blackness.

"You *can* do this, Izzy. You are stronger than you think. Look how much you have already dealt with in your life, and it didn't break you. You survived everything so far. Use that strength now to help heal you." Nick was sitting beside me and I didn't realize he had even entered the room.

"I'm not strong, Nick. I'm scared every day I wake up, not knowing if I can make it through another day. Yeah, sure I can put on a good show and let everyone around me think I'm living the good life. But the reality is every day is a challenge for me to not fall into that spiral that led me to the suicide attempt to begin with." Exhaustion weighed me down and all I could do was lay my head back on the couch and close my eyes.

Nick pulled me close to him. "Let me help you, Izzy. No one said you had to do this on your own. Yes, you have to do the hard work of talking about it, but you don't have to go through it alone."

twenty-nine

Nick and I sat on the couch for what seemed like hours in silence. My thoughts raced with the possibilities and could imagine any logical result. I knew I would have to call my mother and even without questions like these, I dreaded the thought of talking with her. The negativity came through the phone and within minutes my energy was drained from me.

"You have to do it. It's not going to get any easier by waiting." Nick spoke, his lips against my hair. "I'm here with you. You can hang up at any time."

I punched in my parents' number on my phone and listened as it rang. Just when I thought it was going to go to voice mail, my father's voice came over the phone. "Hello?"

"Hi, Dad." I tried to sound cheery.

"Isabelle. What's wrong?"

"Nothing, why?"

"You just don't usually call." I could hear Dad telling my mother I was on the phone. She didn't get on the phone so I figured she didn't want to talk to me as much as I didn't want to talk to her.

"Yeah, well, I have been involved in a little project and needed some family history. Thought you could help me." I wasn't about to tell them about the counseling.

"Okay, what do you want to know?"

I inhaled deeply and exhaled slowly. "In some of my research, I found that Aunt Sarah had a baby. What happened to the baby? I know that Aunt Sarah died shortly after the birth."

Again there was silence. "Let me have you talk with your mother." The phone was handed off and my mother's voice came through. "Isabelle, what do you need?"

"Really? You didn't hear what I just asked Dad?" I sighed and repeated the questions.

"Sarah. She was foolish to think she could face death and come out on the other side without a scratch."

"What does that mean, Mother?" I tried to keep the exasperation out of my voice, but Lord, she could talk in circles without giving a straight answer.

"Yes, she died after childbirth. End of story."

"Mom, what happened to the baby?"

"The baby died with her." Mother's voice was frigid.

"Gram said the baby didn't die." I prodded.

"She's wrong. Your grandmother never could accept the deaths, so she doesn't talk about it." Silence fell between us. "I really need to go, Isabelle."

"Wait." I wracked my brain for something that would not allow the conversation to end.

"What is it?"

"I need my birth certificate for work." I shrugged my shoulders at Nick.

"I already gave it to you. Really, Isabelle, such an important document and you've lost it. Those can't be replaced you know. We'll talk soon." With that, my mother was gone.

I could only shake my head at Nick. She had never given me my birth certificate. The phone had been on speaker so Nick had heard the whole conversation.

"Well, she's wrong about that."

"I know. She never gave me the birth certificate."

Nick chuckled. "No, I meant you *can* replace it. Contact the New Hampshire Department of Vital Statistics. You can request a replacement birth certificate."

I kissed him. "You're a genius."

I grabbed my computer while Nick poured us a couple of glasses of wine. Pulling up the web site for the Vital Statistics of New Hampshire, I found the form to fill out with directions to mail it in. Printing it off, I filled it out and got it ready for mailing out in the morning. "It says it can take two weeks."

"That's nothing. After all these years, you can handle that."

There was nothing more to do at this point, but sit and wait.

I found myself sitting, enjoying the company of Nick, even with minimal talking. We watched TV and snuggled on the couch. Even with the chaos of everything that was going on, I felt a peace. Life was really good.

As time wore on, and TV shows came to an end, Nick kissed me. "It's time for me to go. Are you okay?"

I nodded. "Early morning tomorrow. Hopefully I can sleep."

"I can stay if you want." Nick eyes locked onto mine. I wanted him to stay, but I also needed to be able to do this alone.

I shook my head no. "I'm good. We both need a good night's sleep and have work tomorrow."

"I slept pretty good last night." He winked at me, but pulled me to my feet as he stood.

"Thanks for dinner." I walked him to the door. His kiss was brief, but promising before he turned and leave.

I wandered around the house, picking up and straightening. Shutting off the lights, I stood in front of the balcony door watching the ocean. The waves lapped the land, leaving trails in the sand as it moved back out. The moon glistened off the ocean, deepening the blue color. Funny how I always associated the color of the ocean with Jack's eyes and yet now, Nick's eyes came to mind.

Was I finally moving on? Allowing Nick to see parts of my vulnerability had been a huge feat, and yet it suddenly was worth it. His support had been incredible. He had every opportunity to walk away and yet he was still hanging around. Maybe, just maybe I would eventually be able to open my heart again. Although I knew without a doubt that Jack would always hold my heart.

• • •

Work had me flooded. Upon arriving in the office Wednesday morning, I was greeted with one issue after another. Gayle was tied up in meetings all day, so it had fallen to me to deal with cover art with a typo in the author's name, the wrong color scheme from what we had agreed to and the marketing department breathing down my neck because the budget wasn't finalized.

By the time I sat down at my desk and took a deep breath, it was four o'clock in the afternoon. I had yet to go through the hundreds of emails that came in every day. It was going to be a long night if I didn't get a jump on them. As I scrolled through the emails, trying to pick and choose which ones were the most important to deal with, I found a junk email regarding social media and finding old friends. I stopped on it and reread it.

I had never thought of searching for Jack on social media. Would he be out there? My breath caught in my throat. I put the thought aside and continued on with work…for about five minutes when my mind returned to the idea of searching social media sites. We did it all the time in the publishing business to see if a new author had a web page or was involved in social media to determine what kind of platform they could provide for marketing.

I clicked on the explorer button and pulled up Facebook. I hovered the mouse over the search bar. Feeling like I was doing something wrong, I glanced around me. Jack Riley. I hit search and waited. Three names popped up and there he was, the first one. I would recognize him anywhere. He hadn't changed that much and that smile was the same. I clicked on his name and it took me to his profile. He was no longer in the Air Force. No mention of relationship status. I opened his picture folder and looked through the pictures.

My heart ached. He looked so happy. I toyed with the idea of reaching out to him with a message, but to what end? If the pictures were any indication, he may have a girlfriend, or a wife. I closed out the explorer and went back to my emails. I couldn't do it. It wasn't right to come back into his life and ask that he talk to me. He obviously moved on with his life…which I wanted for him. Why did it hurt so much to think about it then?

I threw myself in to work, answering emails and sending out queries for status on various projects. I sent Gayle an email on the issues I had made decisions on that day to bring her up to speed. I smiled as Jack's face popped into my mind. A recent picture of him. He looked good. And those damn blue eyes and dimples. My heart skipped a beat.

No. This had to stop. I couldn't imagine a life with him. I needed to move forward and leave the past behind. Isn't that what everyone was telling me? Regrettably the only way I could seem to move on was to ignore the past and this damn counseling was not helping me ignore it. It was throwing it my face, a constant reminder to the regrets that I carried.

I forced myself in a different direction. I pulled up new submissions and downloaded one of the manuscripts. I would spend the night reading. At least I could lose myself in another's world for a while, I wouldn't be conflicted in my own. I loved reading submissions, especially the good ones. I would get lost in the story. I stayed clear of the romance and found myself reading the submissions for mysteries and thrillers. A challenge to figure out whodunit.

Over the next few hours I cleaned out my email inbox and felt ready to finally leave the office. Not bad, only 7:30. I hadn't heard from Nick today, which surprised me on one hand, but on the other I had been so busy that I hadn't noticed until it was time to leave and go home. Leftovers for dinner would tide me over while I read this new submission. I hadn't really read the query other than a quick skimming, knowing it was a mystery was good enough for me to at least read the first twenty pages or so.

Dumping my bag inside the door of my apartment, I went and change before heating up some dinner. The quiet of the house hit me harder tonight. Sometimes I relished the quietness, sometimes it just was more of a punch of how lonely I was. Glancing at my phone again, checking for a text from Nick, I sighed not seeing one. I could text him, but I needed this evening to process things. I pulled my laptop on to the couch and juggling my bowl of food and getting the laptop up and running. Finally, I opened Facebook and once again opened Jack's profile. I perused his pictures again; his smile bringing a longing to my soul.

Again, the what ifs hit me. I couldn't go down this road. Instead I pulled up the ancestry site and dug a little deeper into my father's grandparents. Nothing out of the ordinary. Hard working, middle class people. Some veterans. I pulled back up my grandmother's informational sheet and again looked at the children listed: Marie and Sarah. I clicked on Sarah. One child, no name. The date of death was two days after my birth. Was my mother unable to be with my aunt when she died because she had given birth to me? Was that why she resented me so?

I went back and clicked on Marie's informational sheet. Marriage date. No children listed. Perplexed, I pushed the computer aside to finish my dinner. This was absurd. I wouldn't get any answers until I got my birth certificate and could go from there. I didn't even know for sure what hospital I had been born in. No one said and I had assumed it was the local hospital. Finishing the last of my dinner, I pulled my laptop back onto my legs and opened the manuscript.

Just like that I was lost in another world. Twenty pages into it, I knew that if the rest of the book was like the first few pages, I had my newest project to bring to Gayle. It was going to be a long night, but I was determined to finish it before morning.

When the morning sun shined through the balcony windows, I was dozing on the couch. I had drifted off to sleep about four a.m. after finishing the manuscript. I was exhausted, but the sun right in my eyes gave me the nudge I needed to get up. Lovely. Two hours of sleep. Ugh. I stumbled to the kitchen to start the coffee before I headed to a shower. I needed to wake up and get to the office in an hour…okay, if I was being technical I didn't have to be there until eight, but realistically if I showed up that late Gayle would think I was sick.

By 6:45 I was walking out the door with my travel mug filled with my second round of coffee in hand. I walked into the office at seven on the dot. Even when rushing, I was punctual and prided myself on that fact. Something at least everyone could count on from me. Gayle wasn't in yet so I settled in at the computer and emailed her my review of the submission. Another new author, but she had very strong writing. This book would be a hit, I would bet my money.

I played with my phone. Typing quickly, I sent Nick a text. *Hope you had a good night. Talk later?*

Another day in publishing that took my attention away from everything, but what was going on right there. Edits came back from my author and I started going through them. I was thoroughly engrossed in the edits when I heard a knock on the doorway. I looked up to see a young man standing there, holding a vase of flowers.

"Miss, are you Isabelle LaFayette?"

"Yes, that's me." I stood up as he approached my desk.

"These are for you. Have a good day." He placed the

vase on my desk and left. I leaned down and inhaled the scent. It was a mixture of yellow roses with baby breath and a few white carnations. Yellow roses, my favorite, and I inhaled their scent again. I pulled the card from the envelope and read: *Thinking of you. You're not alone through this. Love, Nick.*

My breath caught in my throat. My heart ached at the considerate act on his part. No man had ever given me flowers, and certainly not with a note of support. He was a special man and one that deserved more than I could give. *Don't. Don't push him away.* I berated myself mentally. You did that once before and that didn't work out too well for you.

I snapped a picture of the flowers and sent it to Nick. *They're beautiful. Thank you.*

"Wow, those are gorgeous. Who'd you get in a fight with to deserve an apology?" Gayle's voice had me looking up from my phone.

"No fight. No apology. Just an awesome guy being considerate." I grinned. I literally felt giddy. A feeling I was very unaccustomed to.

"Lucky you, especially with your work schedule. He must be one hell of a guy." Gayle commented.

I contemplated her comment as she walked into her office. Nick never complained about my work schedule. He would send me reminders to eat, make dinner for me and just sit with me on the couch while I read submissions, content to watch TV or read beside me. He was one of the most unselfish men I had met.

I took a step towards Gayle's door. "Hey, mind if I take these edits home and get out of her early tonight? I think I need to cook dinner for him tonight."

Gayle nodded. "Go ahead. If I know you, you'll be

working on edits while you're cooking and probably afterwards too. Give that poor man a little attention through dinner."

"Thanks."

My phone vibrated and I glanced down. *My pleasure.*

I sent Nick a quick text back. *Dinner at 6:30. I'm cooking.*

The return vibration simply showed a smiley face. Another sniff of the flowers and I was out the door. I would have to hit the store first since I rarely cooked and knew there was nothing in the house. I didn't even have a clue what I would be making, but one thing was for sure...it had been a long time that I felt so much anticipation and excitement about a night at home.

With the radio going, I started preparing dinner. How long had it been since I had cooked a real meal? As the aroma of sautéed garlic filled the kitchen, I found myself enjoying the music and the cooking. I prepared the shrimp scampi and put some linguini on to cook. It was 6:25. I expected Nick to walk through the door at any minute.

And there he was. There was a knock and then I heard the door open. "Wow, it smells incredible. What's for dinner?" Before I could answer he came up behind me and kissed me on the neck. "I could get used to this."

I brushed him away. "Beer in the fridge or wine if you'd rather." I already had a glass poured for myself. I drained the pasta and put the finishing touches on the meal just as Nick sat down at the table with a beer in hand.

"So sending you flowers gets me a home-cooked meal...nice." He grinned at me.

I walked over to him, leaned over and brushed my mouth against his. "Thank you again. They were beautiful."

He let me back away as he took a swig of his beer. "Let's eat."

We talked over dinner about work, the book I was editing and his job. He was always very careful about what he said for his work, but I knew how much he enjoyed the work. We worked side by side after dinner to clean the kitchen, although I tried to shoo him out of the way a few times and he wouldn't have it. Finally drying my hands, Nick handed me a freshly poured glass of wine.

We headed to the living room and as I sat down I noticed the bag next to the door. "What's that?"

"Just some clothes for tomorrow. Figured I'd be prepared tonight so I wouldn't have to run home in the morning."

I sipped my wine. "You thought you were staying?" I grinned behind my wine glass.

"Yup. But we're not having sex."

I laughed out loud, not being able to stop it. "Wanna make a bet?"

"You are a nymph. God, woman, learn some self-control." I relaxed at the banter and snuggled close to him.

"Any word about the birth certificate?" he asked.

"Nothing, but I just mailed it a few days ago. I would imagine it's just getting there. Hopefully next week I'll have it back."

"When do you go back to see Mary?"

"Monday evening. I'm not going to have much to tell her about the family tree really. Although I did go back further. Nothing interesting though. No writers in the family."

"None that you know of. Maybe someone was a writer that never got published and somewhere there was a whole stack of manuscripts that no one ever read."

I shook my head. "Nothing that exciting would've happened in my family. My family is the epitome of boredom."

"I don't find you boring…more of a challenge."

I sat up. "Challenge? I'm as boring as they come. Work and more work. Very little play."

"The challenge is in the playing. I'll have you find balance between work and play soon. You're getting there." He winked.

"You're incorrigible."

"I've worked hard to get where I am…an incorrigible man whose one goal in life is to get you to loosen up. I've seen you when you let go. It's a beautiful thing."

Even with butterflies in my stomach, I fought the urge to make sure my guard was in place. I never wanted to completely let go with Nick. I was so afraid I would hurt him. I hid a yawn behind my hand. Damn, it was still early and I hadn't done any editing. "I need to get some work done."

"Really? You can hardly stay awake and you think you're going to work. Izzy, your body needs to relax."

"Honestly, I really would love to just take a hot bath and curl up in bed."

"Go draw the bath. I'll watch TV and when you are out, we'll curl up in bed."

"You sure?" I watched him, looking for some sign that he was upset.

"Yup. Go." He kicked his legs up on the couch as soon as I stood up and reached for the remote.

Maybe relaxing at home wasn't so bad. Nick certainly had no problem making himself at home and somehow there was comfort in that.

thirty

Waking up next to Nick made my mornings so much brighter. We had settled into a routine when he stayed. He would make coffee while I showered and he would jump in as I was getting out. We moved about doing our own thing, getting ready for work and met in the kitchen to grab travel mugs and start our day. It was lacking in conversations in the morning, but it worked for us and there wasn't any lack of kissing going on as we passed each other in our routines.

The weekend was more settled and a less hurried pace. We would linger in bed or over the paper at the kitchen table. We would walk along the beach hand in hand. I never felt an awkwardness whenever there was silence. It was peaceful and it kept me at ease. I found myself still wondering about Jack and would immediately feel guilty for allowing him into my thoughts if Nick was around.

Before I knew it, it was Monday. The work day wrapping up and I would be headed to my counseling session. I hadn't given the birth certificate much thought. I knew without a doubt tonight's session would be a tough one. Mary would be probing about Jack this time since I refused to talk about him last week. I mentally prepared myself for it.

As much as I wanted to refuse to talk about him again this week, I wasn't sure I could get around it for much longer. I pulled into the parking space in front of her building and shut the car off. What a difference a few weeks had made. I no longer felt anxiety coming. There were things I definitely didn't want to talk about, but I wasn't adamant about not opening up. It just was probably a longer process for her to get me to open up. Who knew, maybe all her patients were this difficult.

I walked in and her door was open today. "Come on in, Isabelle."

I entered and glanced out the window, but headed to sit down. Mary noticed and smiled. "How's the week been?"

"Actually really good. Nick surprised me with flowers and he has been so thoughtful about all this…chaos of emotions I have been having."

"Nick? A new friend?"

I realized I hadn't mentioned him before. "I guess. I don't know if I would call it dating, but we're something between friends and more. I don't know how to explain it."

"A relationship." Mary was dry and matter of fact.

"No, not really."

Mary looked pointedly at me. "He gives you flowers, you spend time together, I'm guessing he spends the night occasionally and you don't think it's a relationship? What exactly constitutes a relationship to you?"

I thought about the question. "Well…a commitment of sorts."

"How much of a commitment do you need for it to be a relationship, Isabelle? Nick and you are in an intimate relationship, right?"

"It's just sex."

"Is it? It's sex and he goes home?"

I stood and went to the window. My safe place in this room of questions. "Well, no. We hang out and stuff."

"I hate to break it to you, but you are in a relationship whether you want to be or not. The question is why are you fighting it?"

I turned and faced Mary. "I don't want to hurt him. I don't do relationships. I'm no good at them."

"From what you have said, Nick isn't complaining. He seems very supportive of you and this, how did you put it, chaos of emotions. What are you really afraid of?"

"I can't give him what he wants. I think he knows it, God knows I have told him, but I think he keeps hoping that I will change."

Mary paused her writing. "What is it he wants?"

I shrugged and wandered back to the chair. "More. I was happy with sex without strings, but he wanted more. And I'm not sure how more started happening, but it is some and I will admit I enjoy it, but it's like waiting for the other shoe to drop."

"What is the worst thing that can happen if you open up to him, Isabelle?"

"He will get hurt."

Mary nodded. "So you're not worried about getting hurt yourself, but instead you think you are going to be the one to hurt him?"

I sighed. "I can't explain it. It's what I do. I self-sabotage anything that is good in my life. I ruin it and it's just easier to not let it happen. In the end, Nick is going to get hurt and if it goes on for too long, I will be powerless to stop it. He's a great guy, and I don't want to hurt him." Anguished filled me. I couldn't explain it to someone and even to my ears it sounded nonsensical.

"Who did you hurt before?"

I shook my head no, but Mary just kept her eyes on me. "Jack. It was a long time ago."

"A first love." It wasn't a question.

"My only love. I pushed him away, held him at a distance until he had no choice but to walk away. The hurt in his eyes. I can still see it. To see those eyes filled with hurt and then watch him walk away from me...I can't go through that pain again. I won't go through it again." My tone was fierce and the walls were back up.

"How old were you and Jack?"

I stood again and paced to the window and back. I couldn't sit still. My nerves were on edge and Jack's eyes still haunted me. Talking about it only made it worse. "I was eighteen, he was twenty."

"You were young. We don't always know how to handle things, emotions, at that age. This is about the time you attempted suicide, right?"

I nodded. "That happened a month or two before I met Jack."

"Okay. We talked about how you felt no support at home after the attempt. Did you ever talk with Jack about it?"

I stilled and turned to face Mary. "No, of course not. I know in hindsight I should have. Things may have turned out very different, but I was afraid he would leave." I paused. "Though ultimately I forced him to leave anyway."

"You gave him no choice, Isabelle. You were eighteen. I think maybe you need to cut yourself some slack about the choices you made at that age."

"I can't explain it. It wasn't just the breakup, although it wasn't really a breakup." I closed my eyes trying to collect my thoughts. "My heart was…in sync with his. When he was close to me, I felt alive, more alive than I had been in years."

"Isabelle. Who got hurt the most in this case, with you pushing Jack away?"

"I don't know. I don't know how bad it was for him. Maybe he got over me immediately."

Mary gestured for me to sit. "And you? Did you get over Jack?"

"It doesn't hurt as much when I think about him. For the longest time, every thought caused a physical pain in my chest. I shattered my own heart by trying to save him from…"

"From what?" Mary prodded.

"From the failure I was, the mess I had made of my life." Tears spilled over my lashes. "I didn't have a right to be happy and Jack made me happy. I had to give that up."

"Wait a minute. Why did you not have a right to be happy?"

"Because of the suicide attempt."

Mary laid her paper and pen down on the table next to her. "If someone told you that, they were wrong. And if that is your thought process, you have it wrong, Isabelle. You were eighteen, thought there was no hope and attempted to take your life. That doesn't make you a bad person, nor take away your right for happiness. It makes you someone that was confused and lost, one that needed love and Jack gave you that I take it."

I was at a loss for words. Mary seemed to make it sound so logical, but she hadn't met my mother. "I guess."

Mary leaned forward in her chair. "Isabelle, hear the words I'm saying to you. You have every right to find happiness. You did back then and you do now. You have no reason to feel guilty for hurting Jack. I think your own hurting over Jack's walking away for all these years has been enough and it's time to be okay with it."

"I don't know how." The words were a whisper. "Do you think I don't want to let go of the guilt that weighs me down? Every day I get up and try to just go about my day. I don't get up and intentionally think of Jack and how much I need to feel guilty. Something happens throughout the day and it will remind me of him, and the guilt hits me. It's not every day, but certain times are worse than others. December is hard for me. I miss him so much and the fun I had with him. I truly loved him with all my heart."

"I see your love for him when you talk about him, from the anguish you still feel for what happened. Your heart will heal if you let it. Yes, we get one true love in our life and many people believe that love stays with them forever. However, even if you believe that, it doesn't stop you from loving others. Maybe it won't be as deep as your love for Jack was, but you have the capability to love again and to allow someone to love you."

"Maybe." I wanted to believe her. I wanted to hold on to the thought that maybe I had another chance at love and happiness.

Mary glanced at her watch. "What about the family tree?"

"I worked back like you said. No writers or anyone exciting in my family. Although I did find something a bit odd. I'm not sure how these ancestry sites work, but I was using one to find great-great grandparents and stuff. You know you click on hints they give you and an information page will open up about the person that they find a link to your tree. Well on both my mother and father's information pages, there is no record of them having a child. It's like I didn't exist."

"Those web sites aren't always accurate. It may not mean anything at all. Have you done a search for birth records?"

I shook my head no. "I asked my mother for my birth certificate and she states that she already gave it to me. She didn't, but I've ordered a replacement one."

"Keep digging. You never know and if nothing else, you'll learn something about other members of your family. You never interacted with extended family so I think it's good to learn at least that you have them out there. Who knows, maybe someday you'll want to reach out to some of them and get to know them in person."

"Yeah, it has been kind of fun doing it."

"Good. Open up a little bit and at least acknowledge that you have a relationship with Nick. I know the guilt you are carrying is a heavy load, but we're going to figure out how to lighten that load. I promise you that. We'll meet next week?" Mary had a knack of wrapping up and make me feel like she was shooing me out the door all at once.

I smiled. "See you next week."

As always when I left a session with Mary, my mind was reeling and I needed to process it. Nick seemed to understand this and stayed away on my counseling night. I knew if I needed him, or wanted him to come over, all I had to do was text, yet I never did. Instead most nights, like tonight, I would head to the beach and walk along the water letting the sound of the waves and the smell of the salt water in the air soothe me and help me release the tension.

thirty-one

I had no sooner got home when the skies opened up. Well, there goes my walk. I dashed to the apartment building and still was soaked by the time I reached the enclosure. Processing the counseling sessions wasn't without difficulty. For the next twenty-four hours, as had become the norm, I would mentally replay the sessions and Mary's comments through my mind. Some I would listen to and others I would reject.

Why? Why don't I do relationships well, in my mind? I have come to accept the fact that logic was not my strong suit--in business, yes, but in the matters of the heart, no. I had held on to the past as a shield to protect myself, but in the end I possibly, just possibly, had continued to push everyone else away. It was true. In the process of putting my all into my career, it had become an escape from reality. If I stayed busy enough, my mind couldn't dreg up the past and weigh me down. I could give the illusion of being happy and content.

I was content in my career. I had worked hard and it had paid off. Gayle had taken me under her wing, but I had put in more than a hundred percent. But what was the tradeoff for the seventy to eighty-hour work week? I didn't allow myself time for a life outside of work -- until Nick came along. We had settled into this comfortable routine, and I had found contentment in having him around, but I still held back. I never went to his place. I didn't give him a key to mine. I insisted on having nights to myself. I know Nick wanted more, but I just couldn't give him what he wanted.

I wandered into the bedroom and opened my closet door. Up on the top shelf, in the back corner was an old cigar box held shut with a rubber band. I pulled it down. Carrying it to the bed, I sat and held the box in my lap. I hadn't opened this box in years. It had been painful, and yet for a while I would go through it every night. The rubber band came off easily. Lifting the cover of the cigar box, I closed my eyes for a brief second. Inside, a handful of pictures and some old poems I had written laid there. I picked up the top picture. Jack in his dress uniform, taken on Christmas Eve. He stood feet slightly apart, hands folded behind his back. I smiled as I looked at the picture. Although you couldn't see the blueness of his eyes, the dimples were there as he was enjoying the attention.

I pulled out the next one. Jack and I standing together, his arm wrapped around my waist. That night had been magical. Sitting and talking quietly the two of us, him holding me as I sat in his lap while we talked. That had all ended as soon as he left and my mother started in with her snide remarks. I knew how I had felt about Jack,

I just wish I had known how he felt. I thought he felt the same way and if that was the case, my heart broke all over again for the wasted opportunities and what ifs that never happened.

The next picture I didn't even know had been taken. Jack doing the dishes that night. I was drying and the picture had captured a natural interaction between us. It hadn't been forced between us. Not that things were forced with Nick. If they were it was my fault for holding back. I placed the pictures aside and pulled out the poems. In college I had started writing poetry to pour out some of the emotions that I held in. It was a release of sorts, and yet it never seemed to ease the pain. I had continued writing poetry afterwards.

I sat back against the pillows. I don't know when I stopped. Had it become too painful to write? I searched the recesses of my mind, trying to find out what timeframe it was that I had stopped putting emotion to paper. It was like my mind was blank for a few years. No memories at all. Some of the poems that I had written in college were dark indicating my mind set. Others were written after Jack had left and were of heart break.

I tucked everything back in the box and laid down on the bed. There were no tears, but my heart felt heavy. Mary spoke of letting go of the guilt, but how? Even she didn't seem to have the answer to that. My phone vibrated and I picked it up.

You ok tonight?

Nick. He always seemed to text me when I was feeling the lowest. *Yeah, I guess. Tough session.*

I laid there waiting for his response, playing with the idea to just tell him to come over. I always felt so needy if I wanted him to come over and after all these years, needy wasn't in my vocabulary. Strength. Stubborn. Determined. Those were the words I wanted to use to describe myself at any cost. I pushed the phone aside and laid there staring at the ceiling, replaying Mary's words in my mind.

A knock at the door startled me. How much time had gone by while I laid there daydreaming? My phone indicated the time as 9:30 pm. I should have been working. I had been home for two hours now. I opened the door to find Nick standing there.

"What are you doing here?"

"I figured you might need a hug after a tough session." Nick stepped in and enveloped me in his arms. I leaned against him and soaked in the strength. "Am I interrupting?"

I was hesitant to tell him what I had been doing, but he would see the box of photos anyway if he walked in the bedroom. "Just looking at some old poems and pictures."

"Nostalgic? Or more from the session?" He searched my face. I gave him a weak smile.

"From the session really." Although there was some nostalgia for me, I didn't want him reading into it.

He nodded and waited for my cues. I went to the couch to sit down. "I'm not sure I want to talk about it tonight, but it's just trying to figure out how to get away from the guilt and move forward."

"I can say I understand, but I'm not sure I do. But it doesn't matter if I understand it or not, share what you want or not. Either way, I'm here anyway. I'm not going anywhere."

I blinked back tears once again. This man, sitting here beside me when I was a train wreck, offered support and wanted nothing in return. "I'll be fine. I just get so emotionally exhausted after talking with her."

"Why don't you just go to bed and sleep?"

"I can't sleep. I have a hard time shutting my mind off. I just keep replaying the conversation in my mind. She says some pretty tough things to me." I laughed, try-ing to lighten the mood.

"Which of course you deflect every time." He paused. "Do I get to read the poems?"

I shook my head no. "Of course not. I have never shared them with anyone. They are just from my time in college. Reading them now, they are pretty dark."

"You realize it's just a part of who you were. It doesn't define who you are now."

"Now you sound like Mary."

"Maybe you should listen." Nick intertwined his fin-gers with mine. "You know sharing some of this stuff isn't going to change the way I feel about you."

I wanted to believe that, more than anything. But how do you explain pictures of your first love that you still have? Or poems written about that same love? "May-be at some point I will."

"Do you want me to go?"

"No, I want you to stay with me tonight."

"Then let's go to bed and we can talk in there. Then if you can just drift off to sleep when you're ready. Your eyes are drooping now."

The cigar box on the bed was like a beacon when we walked in the bedroom. I hesitated and then picked it up to return it to the closet. I glanced up to see Nick watch-ing me. "Do you want to see?"

"If you want to share it, but don't feel you have to."

I sat down on the bed and patted next to me for Nick to join me. I once again removed the rubber band and lifted the lid. I pulled out the poems first and handed them to him. Silence was overwhelming as he read through them, not saying a word. One after another he read. After the last one, he simply pulled me close. "Izzy, the emotion you portray. These are good."

"No one has seen them and I had no intention of ever sharing them."

Nick picked them up again. "These should be published. All of them. The dark ones show the anguish you were going through."

I took them from him and put them back in the box over the pictures of Jack. "Maybe someday." I closed the box, placing the rubber band back in place and put in back in its place in the closet. Nick didn't need to see the pictures of Jack. The poems were enough.

"Why did you stop writing?" Nick asked.

I shrugged. "I don't know. I can't even remember when I stopped. I guess when I shut my emotions off, went into survivor mode. Kind of hard to write poetry and you refuse yourself the opportunity to feel anything."

"That is the saddest thing I have heard, Izzy. And I don't mean that negatively. You need to feel, whether it's good, bad or ugly, you need to feel it."

"I guess I got tired of feeling the pain all the time. I needed to protect myself from it, so I shut down emotionally." I crawled into bed. "I can't talk about this anymore."

Nick respected that and held me. I closed my eyes willing my mind to shut off and allow sleep to overtake me.

thirty-two

I awoke before the alarm went off. Glancing over to Nick, sleeping soundly, I crept out of bed and dressed. Once the coffee was made, I went out on the deck to take in the view. The rain from the night before had left a dampness in the air, but the sky was blue and the sun shone causing the ocean to dance like diamonds rolling over the waves. The beach was empty except for the sea gulls looking for scraps to eat.

The blueness of the sky gave me the feel of a new day after the rain, appropriate to my mood. New day, new attitude. It was still early and I could get some editing done before I headed to work. I returned inside for my second cup of coffee and grabbed my laptop. While Nick slept, I worked, losing myself once again in the world of editing and publishing.

As I finished up the work I needed to have done for the office, I set aside the computer and thought about

Nick's comment of having my poems published. I knew enough about publishing to know it wouldn't be a hard thing to do and could even get them in with the press I worked at. I loved reading a new submission that was full of emotion. Emotion that pulled the reader into it and left them feeling like they were right there, that it was written for them, about them. Maybe that could be a fresh path for me to take, a new step towards a positive future.

The morning routine began as soon as Nick came stumbling from the bedroom. "Coffee's all ready." And then just like that we were off our separate ways, starting the day.

I hadn't been at the office long when my cell phone rang.

"Hello?"

"Isabelle Lafayette, please."

"Speaking." I glanced down at the incoming number. Not one I recognized.

"This is Deb from the New Hampshire Department of Vital Statistics. We received your request for a copy of your birth certificate."

"Yes. Is there a problem?"

"Well, we have found a birth certificate with your name and birth date that match, however the mother's name does not match. The maiden name matches, not the first name. Is there a chance Marie would be a nick name she used, or that she would have a different name listed on the birth certificate?"

I was stunned for a moment. The ancestry clue that had indicated my parents didn't have children, yet my aunt had caused me to question everything at once.

"Isabelle?" The voice came through the phone bringing me back to the present.

"Ummm, it's possible she went by Sarah." I had no other options if the maiden name was right.

"There it is. Perfect. I'll get that in the mail to you. Should only be a few days before you get it."

"Thanks, Deb." I disconnected the call and sat in stunned silence. My phone dropped from my hand and hit the desk. The sound didn't even register with me. I couldn't feel my body as my mind raced with questions and the implications of what this could mean. Sarah. This was not what I had expected at all. No wonder my mother…my aunt?…said it had been lost. Was I adopted? That seemed to be the only reasonable explanation. My head started throbbing with the realization of my whole life being a lie. I had no idea who I was or where I belonged.

"You okay? You look like you've seen a ghost." Gayle came into the office, stopping beside my desk.

"Um, yeah, I'm fine. Just a bit of unexpected news." I put my phone down and turned towards my computer.

"Do you need to go tend to anything?" Gayle's concern was touching, but at the moment I just wanted to be alone.

"Nope, I'm fine." The words came out a little sharper than I expected and I sent an apologetic half smile towards her.

She nodded and continued into her office. I sat back in my chair. Sarah was my mother or was it just an error somehow?

Picking up the phone, I typed in a quick message to Nick. *Birth cert has wrong mother's name.*

What do you mean? Nick responded.

They just called. Sarah listed as mother, not Marie.

Who's Sarah?

My mother's sister who died before I was born...or so I was told. Talk later.

It was too much to text and my mind couldn't wrap around it. I pondered calling Gram and Papa and asking them, but they weren't forthcoming the last time I asked them about Sarah. Mother had said Sarah's baby died. My temples started to throb with the start of a migraine. The pounding only increased every time I looked at the computer. I closed my eyes and willed the pain to stop. I could feel the throbbing pain every time my heart beat, as the blood coursed through my veins.

I needed to stop this merry-go-round of emotions. I couldn't explain this to Nick. I called the only person I knew to talk to...Mary. Setting up a time where we could talk for a few minutes, a mini session of sorts, I worked until it was time to leave. Or at least I tried to work. My mind was in overdrive and the headache wasn't helping. By four p.m. I was toast.

"Gayle, I'm not feeling well. I'm going to head home." I stood in her doorway.

She nodded. "You haven't looked well since I got here. Are you sure you are okay?"

"I think it's just a migraine. Nothing that some aspirin and a couple hours of sleep won't fix." How I wished it was that easy.

I arrived at Mary's and she was waiting for me when I walked in.

"I was surprised to hear from when you were just here last night." Mary started.

"Me too, but I didn't know who else to talk with about this." I took a breath and just launched into it. "I received a call today from the birth certificate place in New Hampshire. My mother is not listed on my birth certificate, but her sister instead. The one that supposedly died before I was born."

"Well, that's an interesting wrench thrown into your family tree." Mary watched me. "Obviously, you're not sure how you are feeling about this."

"I asked my mother about Sarah's baby. Remember I found one unnamed child on the ancestry web site? She said Sarah's baby died. Yet, my parents never had children listed on that site. Is it possible that I'm adopted?"

Mary nodded. "Anything is possible, Isabelle. You will need to probably have a conversation with your mother about this." She held up her hand to stop me from protesting. "Process it first, but don't jump to conclusions. And don't let your imagination run away from you on this. This is a speed bump in your life right now. It's how you handle it that will determine how you move forward."

I nodded, inhaled deeply, then exhaled. "Is there any way to track adoptions?"

"You can do a search. Most adoptions are closed so those records would be sealed, but sometimes there are web sites that can help you find someone. The question is, is that the route you want to explore right now? Before talking to your mother and father to get some answers?"

"I honestly don't know. I need to just process it, I guess."

"Don't overthink it. Let things take a natural progression and I have a feeling answers are going to come clearer to you on a lot of things as you continue to work with me and open up about things in your life. Isabelle, it's a process. You aren't going to find answers overnight about things that may have been a family secret for years."

All I could do at this point was either talk to my

grandmother or just wait and see what happened. Of course, Gram had just told me to talk to my mother about Sarah and mother wouldn't tell me anything so that was going to be a dead end anyway. I thanked Mary and headed for home.

Soul searching had become my favorite pastime. It seemed to be a never-ending trip around that merry-go-round. And each time I thought it would slow down or even stop for a little bit, something else came up and I would start spinning again. Maybe a trip home was what I needed. It would be good to see Gram and Papa, but possibly I could get some answers too.

So much for a new day, new attitude. I changed when I got home, donned a pair of dark glasses and headed for the rocky cove. I settled onto the rock and closed my eyes. The sound of the waves crashing onto the rocks swept tension from my shoulders. The smell of the salt air renewed my strength and desire to move forward. I always felt I didn't belong in my family, maybe this was the reason why. How I hated it when people said "there's a reason things happen". I never could understand that because I needed to know the reason, not wait for it to reveal itself.

Okay, so logically if there was a reason for this…what would it be? Obviously if Sarah was my mother and had died a few days after I was born, someone would have had to take me in and raise me. It was logical that her sister would, but why if she didn't want me? Growing up I felt that I was a burden. There was never that joy of you are my child that I imagined there would be with your children. I had imagined that when I had a child, I would hold it and love it. It would be the greatest joy I could have in my life. Yet, that was never portrayed to me by my parents.

God, I was tired. Seven years of carrying all this around with me. Seven years of throwing myself into a career and never taking a day off. As I sat there with the sun beating down on me, I realized I had not had one single day off since I moved to Virginia. This day was long overdue, but it was also time to take more than a day off and use some of the vacation time I had earned. I'm sure Gayle wouldn't object.

The question was when. I didn't want to go back to New Hampshire quite yet. I felt that I was making progress with Mary and my counseling. Heck, I even was enjoying being in a relationship of sorts with Nick. I wasn't ready to handle the confrontation with my parents though and I could acknowledge that. The question became did I look up Jack and try to find closure with that part of my past too. I wasn't sure I was ready to let go of the memories of Jack and I, and yes, maybe even not ready to let go of the pain.

My phone vibrated. *Where are you?* Nick.

At the rocks. What's up?

I tried calling you at work. Said you went home sick.

Migraine. But I went to see Mary too. All's good. I'm going to go back home and sleep for a bit. I replied.

Need anything?

I contemplated this. I needed a lot, but not what he was referring to. *I'm good.* I always felt a twinge of guilt when I replied with something like that. I was good, however, I didn't want him to think I was blowing him off either. But what I really needed was a cup of hot cocoa and a good movie.

thirty-three

The next few weeks flew by in a whirlwind. I had new projects at work that I had taken on and my sessions with Mary were easier and easier to deal with. There wasn't that perpetual exhaustion that followed each session anymore. We had talked about going back to New Hampshire and how I would confront my parents. There was no easy way about it.

The toxicity of the dynamics in my family of origin were damaging. Hearing someone else say to me 'give yourself permission to not allow that in your life' lifted a burden I had carried for many years. I could walk away from the negativity and be okay with it. Gram and Papa would always be there in my life.

I broached the subject of finding Jack, and Mary had no comment on it, which to some extent bothered me. When I finally brought it up again for third time, we had a discussion.

"What is your reasoning for finding him, Isabelle?"

"I want to apologize to him. I acted terrible. He had no idea what I was going through and that was wrong that I didn't talk to him. I'm not expecting anything in return. Honestly, I think I'll be okay just seeing him and moving forward."

"What about Nick? Have you talked with Nick about this?"

I shook my head no. "Why would I talk with Nick?"

"Well, he has an investment in this. What if you go to New Hampshire and see Jack, and things make an unexpected turn when you realize you are more in love with Jack than Nick. Is that fair to Nick to leave him hanging, waiting in Virginia for you?"

"It's not going to be like that." I once again headed to the window. My spot of choice when the questions pushed me beyond my comfort zone.

"Isabelle, how do you feel about Nick?"

"I care for him deeply. I don't want to hurt him. Things are comfortable between us."

"Care for him. Is that love to you and your just afraid to use that word?" Mary prodded.

"Love? I'm not sure I would recognize love if it hit me in the forehead."

"Is it just friendship you feel for him?" Mary was not letting this go and I fidgeted by the window.

"No. It's more than that. I look forward to the nights he is at the apartment waiting for me. There is a comfort in having him there. He takes my breath away sometimes with his acts of kindness to me, the support he gives… and yeah, he's good looking."

"But it's not like you were feeling when you were with Jack?"

I stared at her. I didn't want to compare the two. "It's apples and oranges. They're different. I'm different than I was when I was with Jack. I'm older, wiser I'd like to think."

"Right. That's my point. You were in love with Jack. But I think you're in love with Nick too and it feels different and you fight anything associated with the 'L' word. Have you and Nick talked at all about how you feel? Or are we avoiding that conversation?" Mary tried hard to keep a smile off her face. Over the past few months of working together, she had gotten to know me quite well and would call me out on many things I tried to avoid.

"Why does it have to be labeled? Why do we have to call it love, or a relationship?"

"What I find ironic in all this…" Mary paused and waited for me to sit down. "You, in all these sessions we have had, the underlying theme has been you just want love. You wanted love when you a child, when you were a teenager and whether you want to admit it now or not, you still crave someone to love you. Yet, you balk at even allowing that to happen."

"I wouldn't say I balk…" I trailed off.

"No? What do you call it?"

"Self-preservation." I shrugged. "I don't know. I fell in love with Jack and shattered my heart when I made him leave. I don't want that pain again."

"Who says you'll have that pain again? You're a different person now. You are a different person from just three months ago." Mary stopped. I waited, knowing she wasn't done. "I'm amazed at how far you have come over the months we have been working together. You have done the hard work and fought through the past. You've talked about it and I think you have put it behind you… at least some parts of it. But you haven't let go of Jack."

I shook my head no. "I'm not ready to, but I think that's why I need to see him. Maybe that would bring closure to it all."

"Or open the wound again." Mary was blunt, but honest. I knew that she wanted me to look at it from all angles.

"Can it hurt any more than it already has?"

"Probably not. Maybe it will. But in the meantime, it's not just you and Jack that could get hurt. What about Nick?"

"What if I had Nick's blessing to go and find Jack?" I was unsure about mentioning it to Nick, but wanted to see Mary's reaction.

"Then if he gives you his blessing, I would say he loves you very much and you're a fool to let that go." I felt sucker punched. Of all things, that was not what I was expecting from her. I didn't know how to respond and just sat there looking at her. "I think that got your attention. Give some thought to that, Isabelle, before you move forward with your decision to find Jack."

"Fine." The word wasn't defiant, it was defeat. I knew she was right. "I'll talk to Nick."

This was not a conversation I wanted to have with Nick. These days, Nick always had dinner ready when I came home from counseling. It had become a routine and one I normally looked forward to. Tonight, I was dreading it. Not that I needed to have this conversation tonight, but I wanted to make plans about going to New Hampshire. And if the truth was told, I needed to know how he felt about me. I had let love slip by when I didn't tell Jack I loved him. Was this love though?

I came through the door of the apartment to find Nick sitting on the couch. "Hey." I didn't smell anything cooking for dinner.

"How was tonight?" Nick made no effort to move. I was uneasy and suddenly on guard.

"It was good. I think I'm getting better at talking about things." I sat down next to him. "What's going on, Nick?"

He sighed. "I figured we could order a pizza for dinner. I didn't feel like cooking."

"Okay." I waited.

"I feel we're in limbo, Izzy. I told myself a hundred times I wasn't going to push you, but I'm unsure where we stand. You know I want more. I know you're guarded. But we can't do this dance forever."

I smiled. "Mary and I were having this same conversation today. I know we need to talk about how things are and where we are headed. I've been scared to have this conversation with you because I don't know how to describe how I feel."

"Izzy, I told you I would always be here for you...and I will. I'm not going anywhere, but I do need to know if we are caught in this weird zone between friendship and lovers, or if it's more."

"Nick, I don't know. I'm being honest and I don't want you to take that the wrong way. I have been so focused on how to move forward from my past and just dealing with that...I know I haven't been easy to be with. You have been incredible in your support." I wanted to say 'and love', but Nick had never said he loved me. And neither had Jack. Maybe I wasn't the type of person men fell in love with.

"Don't even say but..." Nick broke in.

I laughed. "I wasn't going to. I can't tell you enough how much I appreciate you being here. I look forward to coming home from work and spending time with you. Hey, I'm even used to you spending the night."

Nick shook his head and chuckled. "No, you definitely haven't freaked out lately when I'm here in the mornings. Izzy, you know I care for you."

"I know. I care for you too." I couldn't help but wonder if when we said we cared if it was code for something else. If he loved me, why wouldn't he just say it? "How do you feel about me going back to New Hampshire for a visit?"

"I think it would do you good. You need to spend some time with your grandparents and you need to deal with the birth certificate issue. Do you want company?"

"Don't be upset, but no. I need to do this myself."

"I get it. I'm not upset."

I took a deep breath. "How would you feel if I looked up Jack?"

"Jack? The guy you were heartbroken over?" I nodded. Nick ran his hand over his face and sighed. "You do what you have to, I guess."

"Seriously, Nick. I need to know how you feel about this. I just need closure. I need to apologize to him."

"You never talk about him to me. I know he's a ghost between us and I don't know what to think of it. But if this is the reason you can't fully be invested in us, then go do it." I could tell by the look on his face he wasn't happy about it.

I stood and walked into the bedroom. It was time to have this out. I grabbed the cigar box from the closet and returned to the living room. I opened it up and held it out to him. He was hesitant about taking it, but finally took it from my hands, his eyes never leaving mine.

"You read the poems, Nick. Here though, look at

these pictures." I pulled out the pictures of Jack and me. I couldn't help but smile. "These were Christmas Eve. This is Jack. Look at us, we were babies really. So young and stupid. I didn't know how I was supposed to feel or act. I had just come home from college after the suicide attempt when I met Jack."

Nick flipped through the pictures. "You looked happy."

"I was. And finding Jack isn't about trying to find that happiness again. There was a lot unsaid, and after seven years of never acknowledging what happened not just with Jack and I, but at college and how my family treated it. After finally getting it out and being able to talk about it, Jack deserves to know why I treated him like I did. It's not about trying to find that kind of love I had then, it's about..." I trailed off.

Nick put the pictures back in the box and handed it to me. "It doesn't matter what it is about. And I don't say that to cut you off. I mean it. It doesn't matter. You need to do what you feel is best for you. I'll be here when you get back. You need to know one thing though." He reached for my hand and held it. "My heart is involved here. I have held off telling you that because I was afraid you couldn't handle hearing it. You are so skittish around anything that involves your heart. Izzy, go to New Hampshire, find Jack if you have to but know that I love you."

My hand tightened around his. Those words I had longed to hear. A tear rolled down my cheek. "I don't know what love feels like anymore, Nick, but I know you have found your way into my heart through the cracks, and slowly the walls are coming down by your support." It wasn't a proclamation of love, but it was as close as I could come at this point.

"Whatever happens, Izzy, promise me that we'll talk

about it face to face. If Jack comes back into your life and you need to move on away from me, tell me."

"I promise."

The days flew by after that conversation. I arranged with Gayle to take a week off from work, a vacation that I hadn't had in seven years. Gayle knew I was headed to New Hampshire to deal with some family issues, but never asked any details. I was grateful for her support of me taking the time I needed. She assured me that if I needed more time, it wouldn't be an issue.

thirty-four

I arrived in New Hampshire. Peering out the airplane window, it became apparent nothing had changed. The weather was overcast -- fitting for what I was feeling at the moment. The next few days were going to be difficult, by far the most difficult I had yet to encounter through this whole counseling journey.

First stop was my grandparents. They were the only ones who knew I was coming. I had started this path of enlightenment and healing six months ago. There had been obstacles at every turn and I hadn't been prepared for the heartache this would cause me, or for the information that had come to light. Apparently, my path had been chosen for me a long time ago and unbeknownst to me I had made decisions based on lies and falsehoods that left me filled with regret and a desire to be able to redo my life and the choices I had made.

Once I was off the plane, and a rental car procured, I started out on the familiar roads that I had left behind me almost eight years ago. I took a detour through the capital and stop at the park to reflect on how much everything had changed. Everything, me included. I had five days minimum here. If I wanted to stay longer, I could change my plane ticket, but for now five days was more than enough to do what I had to do.

On the road again, I drove through the idyllic towns that I had grown up around, past my high school, past the pizza place where Jack and I went on our first date, and on to my grandparents. Memories came in flashes -- some good and some painful. High school had been a roller coaster ride for me. Good days and bad days, battling depression that no one knew about. I had played the part of the happy-go-lucky cheerleader, friends with everyone, yet not close to anyone. I looked back and have no idea how I made it through those four years. When everyone talks about high school being the best four years of your life, I wonder who they were talking about. Teenagers are gawky, awkward and life is not easy at that age. If that is the best years of your life, shoot me now.

Though I could honestly say they weren't the worst four years of my life. Those would have been the time in college leading up to the suicide attempt and the time right after. It wasn't a four-year span, but it seemed to last a lifetime when I was in the midst of it. It amazed me how I survived it.

Jack.

Jack had been my reason for putting one step in front of the other. It had been a short time that we were together, but he would never know how much he brought me to life again.

In the throes of feeling completely isolated even in my family, Jack had reached out and held me…held my hand and my heart. I wish I had been brave enough at that point to tell him I loved him. He should have known. He should have known what I was going through. If I had had the courage, maybe, just maybe I would have learned that he wasn't going to run from it. He may have been that rock I needed to keep me grounded. Years of regret piled up in me and my throat constricted as it did when I fought to hold back tears.

I drove into my grandparents' driveway and pulled myself together. Jack couldn't be my focus right now. I had other things to deal with. But now, all I wanted was to wrap myself up in my Gram and Papa's arms and listen to some Louis Armstrong with my Papa. I grabbed my bag and before the back door had shut, my grandparents were out the door to greet me. I dropped my bag and threw my arms around them.

"I have missed you guys so much." Tears welled in my eyes as I realized I had unwittingly cut them out of my life too.

"Izzy. We're so glad you are here. Have you eaten?" Gram grabbed my arm and pulled me towards the house. "Papa get her bag."

"Yup, leave me to do the heavy work." He grumbled as he winked at me. "I want to hear all about the famous authors you work with."

"No one famous, or that you would know, Papa. But I do have some good stories about some of the stories we have rejected."

Within minutes, I was seated at the table, a plate in front of me of Gram's homemade apple pie and a glass of Moxie. Moxie. I hadn't drunk that in years, not since I moved. It was Papa's favorite and I had developed a love for it. Moxie and Louis Armstrong, the best things in life my Papa ever gave me. I grinned at them.

Gram proceeded to fill me in on the local news. People I once knew, who was married, divorced, had kids and of course who had died. Gram loved a good funeral. I listened and immediately was transported back to my childhood. I would spend hours, days with my grandparents. In the summertime when school wasn't in session, I would spend overnights here, sometimes two or three nights in a row. My parents never seemed to mind and I was more at home here than at my own home anyway.

"Well, Izzy…" Gram was looking at me. "How's the pie?"

I looked down at my empty plate. "Delish as usual. You make the best pie and I have missed it so much…as well as you and Papa. I can't believe I haven't been back to see you for almost eight years. I wish you would have come to visit me."

"Well what was the point of us coming down there, with your work schedule and all? You wouldn't have been home to spend any time with us." Papa delivered the sarcasm with a smile.

"I would have taken time off for you." I fluttered my eyelashes at him and Gram batted her hand at me.

"You two knock off all that nonsense." She took my empty plate and rinsed it off. "Come on, let's go out on the patio."

Their screened-in patio held so many memories for me. I had spent hours here playing with the kittens they always seemed to have while they sat in lawn chairs, Papa smoking his pipe. I sank into a chair and exhaled. Home. This was home for me.

"Well, child, are you going to leave us in suspense or are you going to spill it?" Gram always was the impatient one.

"I haven't seen them yet. I came straight here. I needed to get my thoughts together before I confronted them." Once I had learned that Sarah had been my mother, not my aunt, I had been so hurt and angry. It had taken Nick days to figure out how to get through to me. Even my counselor had been at a loss on how to help me cope with the overwhelming anger that resided in me.

Gram and Papa hadn't been surprised that I found out. Their apologies ebbed the angry flow, at least towards them, though I still didn't understand why no one told me. This was a huge thing in my life and yet true to form, this family hid away facts that might appear to the outside a blemish in their perfect little world.

"Izzy, you need to be calm when you talk to them." Papa reiterated. He had said this countless times to me in the past few weeks.

"I know, but I'm not sure how calm I can be if she... mother...or is she my aunt...takes her holier than thou attitude. She's so hypocritical." I took a deep breath. I didn't want to get worked up quite yet. "Anyway, I'm not going to go see them until tomorrow. So let's just enjoy tonight and not talk about it."

Gram cleared her throat. "When this is done, you won't be coming back here, will you?"

Once again tears threatened to spill. "I don't know, Gram. I really don't. I don't think I will be back to see them, but you and Papa...I want you in my life. I don't blame you for what happened."

Papa cleared his throat. "I don't understand why you don't blame us. Not that I want your anger directed at me, but honestly we didn't tell you either."

I nodded. "I know and I was angry at you guys at first. But in the end, you never treated me any different. You treated me like your grandchild, which I am regardless of whether I am Marie's child or Sarah's." I paused. "I know how my mother, or Marie, whoever can be. Once she's is determined no one says something, she's not crossed. Let's face it, if you were to cross her she would have cut you out of our lives and I would have missed out on have grandparents. I see it that in the end you were there for me no matter what."

"You're right. You are our grandchild regardless of who the birth certificate says is your mother. Just remember, your mom took you and raised you, even if she didn't do it in the best way--her intentions were good."

I shrugged. I honestly could care less about my mother's good intentions. She was wrong. No ifs, and, or buts. Good intentions would have been showing she loved me. Taking me in because her sister died, great. But treating me poorly all these years because she was mad that her sister died and blamed me for it...I didn't know that for a fact, but that is the deduction I had made through all this mess. Nick told me not to jump to conclusions until I had talked to my parents, but my mind was a runaway train with the extent of what my mother's reasons could have been for the way she had treated me over the years, especially after the suicide attempt -- or 'when I didn't feel good' as she put it if it ever came up.

"Where's Louis, Papa?" I changed the subject.

"Same place you left him." He puffed on his pipe, making no effort to move.

I ran up the stairs to the house and pulled out the album that was my favorite. Soon Louis' voice filled the speakers. I turned the volume up so it could be heard out on the patio. How I had missed Ole Satchmo's gravelly voice. Papa was rocking away when I came back to the patio. He rocked in time to the music and puffed his pipe.

"Just like old times." Gram smiled as she picked up her knitting. Silence between us was filled with the sounds of the saxophone and singing. I closed my eyes and let the music take me away. I mentally made myself a note to pick up a digital version of this album so I could listen to it as I walked on the beach.

As the album finished, and we waited for the next album I had placed on the record player to drop down, Duke Ellington, another favorite, Gram broke in. "What are you plans beyond tomorrow, Izzy?"

"Visiting with you and Papa, and maybe look up an old friend." Duke's voice filled the patio. "I'm only here for five days."

"Anyone I know." Gram never raised her eyes off her knitting, but I felt the fishing line pull. Gram never missed a chance to get some gossip.

"I don't know. And I'm not going to say, Gram." Papa chuckled. I had a hint of apprehension, like there was something they knew that I was unaware of, or was it that they knew me too well.

The music again took over the conversation and we sat in silence. After going through a few more albums that included Ella Fitzgerald and Glenn Miller, the music stopped. Silence filled the air around us and yet it wasn't awkward at all. I glanced between Papa and Gram. Gram knitting away and Papa humming as he finished his pipe. It was almost as if time had stood still for this moment. A reminder of happy childhood memories. Memories that couldn't be tainted by anything or anyone. This was a part of my life that had always been stable and filled with love. I just seemed to forget that for a while in the midst of the crushing chaos that had consumed me too many years.

thirty-five

I awoke to the aroma of bacon wafting through the air. Bacon and coffee. My two favorite things. I laid in bed and listened to my grandparents bantering downstairs. How those two could still flirt after all these years was a testament to their devotion to each other. I dressed quickly and pulled my hair back in a ponytail and flew down the stairs.

"Morning." I walked into the kitchen. Papa was beside the stove finishing the bacon while Gram was setting the table. A stack of pancakes was on the table, fresh from the griddle.

"I was beginning to think I would be eating all this bacon myself." Papa placed a plate full of bacon on the table. "About time you pulled yourself from that bed."

"I admit I never sleep in like this, but I slept so good last night." I poured coffee in three mugs and placed them on the table. "I haven't slept that good in a long time."

"Coming home is always good for the soul." Gram quipped.

I washed dishes after breakfast and cleaned up the kitchen. I knew I was stalling, but I wasn't in any hurry to get to my parents' house.

"You sure you want to do this alone?" Gram asked from behind me.

I nodded. "I have to. This isn't you and Papa's battle."

She said nothing, just simply folded me into her arms. "We love you, Izzy. Know that we have always loved you."

"I do know that." I kissed her cheek. "And I love you guys so much."

I took a deep breath and headed for the car. I would be staying at my grandparents the whole time I was here so I needed nothing, but myself for this excursion. My nerves were frazzled and even the radio grated on my nerves for the short ride. I would flip it off, and then immediately turn it back on because the silence was deafening. Pulling into my parents' driveway…parents? That seemed such an odd statement to me now. What did I call them? It didn't matter because I had a feeling that after today, ties would be broken and there would be no reason for me to ever talk to or see them again.

I walked to the door, taking in the house. Nothing had changed in seven years. Same flowers out front, the gardens impeccable as usual. The garage was clean and swept out. I stopped at the doorway. Do I knock? Just go in? After almost eight years of being gone, I opted for knocking.

The door opened and shock registered on my father's face when he saw it was me. "What are you doing here?"

I stepped into the house. "Just here for a quick visit."

"Where's your stuff?" My father looked out to the garage. "Is it in the car?"

"No. I'm staying at Gram and Papa's. I got in last night."

He nodded and gestured to the living room. "Your mother is in there."

I took a deep breath and stepped into the living room. Mother stood and gave me a hug. "What a surprise." The tone was unreadable in her voice. Was she displeased by the surprise or genuinely happy to see me?

"I'm sure. It's been a while." I looked around the room. "Not much has changed here though, has it?"

"No need to change anything when it works." And there she was. The prim and proper, distant mother I grew up with. Everything in its place.

I sat down. There was no easing myself into this conversation. "So, what is it I'm supposed to call you these days?"

My parents looked at each other. "What do you mean?" Mother finally spoke.

"Is it mother and father, mom and dad, aunt and uncle?" I watched carefully as the words registered with my mother. "As it turns out, one can replace their birth certificate if their so-called parent doesn't want them to have it."

"Isabelle. You don't have any idea what you are talking about." Mother spoke, yet father was strangely quiet through this exchange.

I glanced over to him and his eyes were downcast, tears trailing down his cheeks. "It's time, Marie."

"Did you even adopt me? Or was it all just kept hush and nothing was done legally?"

"Isabelle, it's really not like that." Her father spoke, but his words were quiet. He looked like he aged ten years in the two minutes of conversation.

"Well, do fill me in. What was it like? I grew up in a household where I felt unwanted and couldn't figure out why I didn't fit in." I pointed at mother. "You acted like you hated me, especially after the suicide attempt. And yes, I said suicide attempt. I wasn't not feeling well, I tried to kill myself."

"Isabelle, you're being a little dramatic. Just calm down and we'll explain." My mother's mouth was pinched in her disapproving way.

"Dramatic? This is my life. A life that up until just a few months ago had been a lie, all a lie." My head pounded with the rush of blood my heart was pumping out. My heart rate I couldn't slow down. I clenched my fists in my lap. I wanted to explode at her icy stare.

"Your life wasn't a lie. You had parents that loved you." Mother glanced at Father and back at me. "We do love you."

"You have a funny way of showing it. Whose idea was it to keep it quiet and not tell me that Aunt Sarah was really my mom?"

"Oh, that's rich." My mother stood, anger in her face, her back rigid. "A mother who could have cared less about you. She knew she probably wouldn't survive child birth, but she purposely got pregnant anyway because she was a selfish bitch that just wanted a child. She didn't think about the rest of us and how it would impact our lives."

"Marie, that's enough." Father finally spoke. I glanced at him as he stood and came to sit next to me on the couch. "Isabelle, I never wanted you to feel you didn't belong here. You were my daughter from that moment I held you in my arms and knew I would be raising you. I never thought of you as anything but my daughter." Tears flowed again down his cheeks. I held his hand. He was at least sincere.

"Of course we thought of you as our daughter." My mother's voice on the other hand was still cold and gave the impression this was all just a nuisance.

"I remember hearing you talk to Dad. You were mad about me ruining your career, having to raise me. I didn't understand then, but you didn't want to take me in, did you?"

"I will admit it was your father's idea for us to raise you. I was angry and hurt that Sarah had done this without thought of the consequences. And you know, there are consequences for your actions. Look at you…"

"No. We are not looking at my life. We are looking at the lies you have told me and the fact that you are not my mother." I hung on to Dad's hand for dear life. I wanted to throttle this woman standing before me trying to turn this around to every bad thing I had done in my life.

"I never lied to you. I never came out and said I gave birth to you." Mother shrugged and sat back down.

"Are you kidding me right now? Lie by omission. I asked you about Sarah's baby and you said the baby died. You lied to me. I didn't die."

"Well, technically Sarah's baby did, because that day that Sarah died you became our child. You were no longer Sarah's baby."

"You cold-hearted bitch." I turned to my father. "Thank you for loving me through the years like you did, although you should have stood up more for me with her." I pointed at Mother. I kissed him on the cheek and stood.

"You on the other hand, have been a resentful, bitter, old lady. I want nothing more to do with you. You never showed me a bit of love when I needed it. You treated me with contempt, something you were ashamed of."

"Well, you did your best to shame us pulling that stunt at college." Mother sat in the chair stiff as a board.

"Stunt? Again it was not a stunt. I tried to kill myself. Let those words register with you because that is the fact of the matter. Listen to it again. I tried to kill myself. Do you understand the implication of those words or are you too stuck in your high and mighty ways, hiding from society anything you think might be dirty laundry?" I shook my head. "I almost feel sorry for you.

"You'll never understand how to give love unconditionally, although you have a living example that puts up with all your crap and loves you anyway. Why else would Dad still be here with you? But no more. This ends now. I will no longer be the focus of your bitterness. Deal with it. My mom, Sarah, died. Your sister died. At some point you need to face reality and realize none of it was about you. Sarah died because she loved and wanted a child so bad she put her life at risk. That's the kind of love a mother shows her child. You only focus on what her death did to your life. What about the impact she had on your life when she was alive? Did she make it fuller? Were you jealous of her then? I missed out on knowing my mother because you never talked about her. I should've known what kind of person she was and you took that away from me."

My mother stared straight ahead, not making eye contact. Rigid and cold. I shook my head.

My father stood and gave me a hug. "I'm sorry, Izzy."

In all my years growing up, my father had never called

me Izzy. That was the breaking point for me. A moment of tenderness and love that was twenty-five years too late.

I hugged him close.

"Don't let anger run your life," he whispered. "Look what it does to people." He gave me another tight hug.

I nodded. It was true, anger had turned my mother into a bitter lady, not someone I wanted to become. Without a word, I left the house.

I didn't look back as I drove away. This was a chapter that was closed. Maybe in time I would communicate with my father, but my mother had closed that door herself, and as far as I was concerned, it was locked.

When I arrived at my grandparents, I just sat in the car trying to collect my thoughts. I realized a web of lies destroys all that come in contact with it.

thirty-six

I had no sooner driven into my grandparents' driveway when a car came up behind me. My father stepped out-- or did I call him *uncle?*

I shook my head to clear the negative thoughts. He wasn't the real problem.

With a sigh, I opened the door and stepped out to meet him.

"Izzy, we need to talk." He spoke softly.

"Hasn't everything been said?"

He shook his head. "There's more your mom doesn't even know."

"Mom? Or your wife?" I was being snarky because I knew exactly who he meant, but I couldn't help it.

"Isabelle, she's been the only mother you had. Yes, we should have told you, but we didn't."

I gestured toward the house and saw Gram looking out the window.

"Let's sit on the porch. Your grandparents don't know this either."

What? How many secrets did my family have?

Fear clenched at my heart; my hands clammy at the thought of what I would hear. Dad didn't say a word as we both settled into chairs. I sat silently waiting for him to start.

He squirmed, trying to get comfortable, clearly ill at ease at with what was coming. "You found out Sarah was your mom." He paused.

I nodded and waited.

"But your father wasn't listed."

I clenched my hands together. "No. It was left blank on the birth certificate."

"I know. Sarah didn't want anyone to know, and I'm asking you for the sake of your mother -- Sarah--to continue to keep this secret." He glanced over his shoulder at the door. "Sarah didn't want anyone hurt and she knew more problems would come out if it was known."

I stared at him. Willed him to just say it. My mind raced and I could come up with no one that I could imagine to be my father.

"You have to understand, the relationship between Marie and Sarah was strained at best. Marie was so judgmental of Sarah's decisions and jealous."

"Jealous? Of what?" I interrupted.

"Your mom, Marie, had no self-confidence. She wished she could be more like Sarah, believe it or not." Dad stared off, seemingly lost in memories.

"For the love of god, Dad, just tell me who my father is." I couldn't stand it.

He reached for my hand and just looked at me for a moment. "Izzy, *I'm* your father."

"Are we continuing with this charade?" Irritation

laced my words. I had enough. My emotions were frazzled and I couldn't take another lie.

"No, Izzy. I made a mistake. Sarah and I did. We didn't mean for it to happen..." He trailed off. I just stared at him, shaking my head. My stomach turned and I fought back the nausea. My mind raced to try and process all that was being said to me, and yet I couldn't seem to grasp the full reality of dysfunction in this family. "Say something," he pleaded.

"No one knows?"

He shook his head. "I told Sarah we would raise you, but no one could know about her and I."

"How did this happen?" My world had collapsed and the dynamic I thought I figured out was gone just like that. My mind whirled.

"Marie and Sarah had a fight. I knew Marie had been unreasonable and I went to check on Sarah. I was worried about her."

"So sleeping with her was just to comfort her?" I stood and paced the porch.

"It wasn't like that. It happened. I'm not making excuses, and I won't blame Sarah. I take responsibility for that night."

"You were always my father and you let her belittle me, make my life miserable." It was a statement, not a question, yet I couldn't believe it. "You never stood up for me...your own daughter."

Reality of the situation washed over me and yet I had no words to even describe the depth of my emotion. I couldn't even pinpoint the exact reaction -- rejection? Sadness? I needed time to process all of this. I was already on the emotional roller coaster from the confrontation with my mother, my aunt, whoever she was, and then the man I had come to think of as my uncle, not my dad actually turned out to be my biological father.

"Izzy, I know I haven't handled things right. I didn't know what to do. Sarah wanted you to be in a good household. She truly believed that Marie would treat you like her own child."

I shook my head. "But she never wanted children."

I wanted to scream and hide away from everyone at this point. I was so tired of all my emotions being all over the place, pushing and pulling at me, giving me hope and causing frustration. I paced the porch, feeling my father's eyes on me. He was silent, waiting for me to speak.

"No one else knows this?" I finally asked.

"No. Sarah wanted it that way." Dad sat back in the chair. "Izzy, will you keep the secret?"

"I can hardly wrap my head around all this. Do you know that I have felt so unwanted all my life? I felt I didn't belong in the family...anywhere." I sank into a chair. How could I ever get past all this dysfunction and find a normal life for myself. I trusted no one and my heart was locked up tight. There was no room for anyone to get in--not even a hope of a chance in this lifetime.

Gram and Papa were waiting in the living room when I entered the house. I had never held anything back from my grandparents, and yet I felt a sense of guilt at the weight my father had just put on my shoulders in keeping this secret from them. I walked in and the tears fell. I couldn't hold it back any longer. Within seconds I was enfolded into my grandparents' arms. We stood there, the three of us, me in the middle with my grandparents just holding me. I let myself go. Tears of grief, anger and despair flowed from me.

"Healing tears, Izzy. It's all good." Gram's voice registered through my broken mind. I was helpless to think clearly. "Come on, let's sit down."

They led me to the couch and the three of us sat, me flanked by Gram and Papa, my protection and safety net. "I need to know about her."

"Sarah was a spitfire, just like you." Papa started. "She held her own and was always determined to do things herself, even when she was nothing but a wee toddler."

"We had our hands full when she got older. Rules she felt were made for breaking." Gram jumped in. "Lord, that girl made me cry a lot while she was in her teenage years. I was so worried she would get hurt, but she always made life look easy. And happy. She was so happy all the time."

Hours went by as I learned of my mom. Her likes and dislikes, her petulance when things didn't go her way and her endless hours of teasing her sister. "Back then, Marie adored her sister. She was a year younger and followed her around everywhere. Although they were night and day. Sarah a free spirit and Marie more rigid and controlled. I think Marie was always a little jealous of Sarah and the way she had no cares in the world. Marie became very protective when we found out about Sarah's hemophilia and how severe it was. Sarah, on the other hand, refused to let it stop her and even seemed to challenge life to see how far she could push it."

"Why did she get pregnant, or did she get pregnant on purpose?"

Gram sighed. "Yes, she got pregnant on purpose. Besides the hemophilia, Sarah had some other medical issues that no one knew about. She refused to talk about them and refused any kind of treatment. She felt she wouldn't be around forever and wanted more than anything to have a child. She wanted to hold you in her arms before she died…and she did. You were the greatest gift in her life and although she only had you for a short time, she wouldn't have changed it."

My mother had given birth knowing she wouldn't be raising me. "But why was Mother so angry then if she knew she would be raising me?"

Papa cleared his throat. "Marie has always been very rigid. She was first angry when Sarah refused to tell her about her medical issues. We don't know for sure what was going on, as Sarah asked her doctor to keep that part confidential even after her death. But after she learned Sarah was pregnant and that the outcome probably wouldn't be a positive one, Marie stopped talking to her sister. They eventually started talking again right before you were born, but by that time the damage was done. Sarah was hurt and felt that Marie selfishly wasted the last of her time with her sister. She even came to Gram and me to see if we would raise you."

"I wish you had." The words sounded bitter even to me.

"We really thought Marie and Darryl were the right place for you. I honestly thought that as you got older, and as you were more and more like your mom, Sarah, that Marie would cherish that. Unfortunately, it had the opposite effect on her. The more you reminded her of Sarah, the more distant she became. We tried to talk to Darryl about it, but he just told us we didn't understand the way Marie handled her grief."

"That certainly explains as I got older the more distant she became to me, and cold. I never could understand how cold she was towards me." I stared into space. "It's done now. I don't want to dwell on that. It's time to move away from the negativity in my life. I want to know everything about Mom, and pictures…do you have any pictures of her that I can have?"

"Of course. We'll pull some out while you are here and go through them. You can have anything of hers that you want. I also have some letters for you that she wrote you at the end of her pregnancy. I never told Marie about the letters. I was waiting for the right time to give them to you, but there never seemed a good time since you didn't know."

I sat in awe listening to my grandparents talk of the antics of Sarah. They came alive when they talked of her. My heart warmed even more with love for them. They were parents that showed their love for their children and Sarah they obviously had missed dearly over the years. She had been gone twenty-five years. The impact of that hit me. They still missed her like it was yesterday.

As I crawled into bed later that night, my mind reeled with the events of the day. As I started to process it, exhaustion overtook me. I spent the next few days with my grandparents pouring over countless photo albums of Sarah. I found a few that I wanted to frame and took them with me. Gram had given me the letters and I had yet to open them.

My last night with Gram and Papa, I used the excuse of an early day to fly back to Virginia to go to bed early. I sat in bed with the letters in my lap. There were three of them. They were each marked to be opened on a specific day: Izzy knows, Wedding Day, just when you need me. Okay, well two were fair game for me to open. She would never know if I opened all three, but I knew I would save the one for my wedding day for that day…if there ever was one. I told myself, if that day never came I would open it when I turned forty.

I grabbed the letter marked *Izzy knows*. The handwriting was similar to Mother's, yet a bit more flowy. I opened it and pulled the paper out.

Isabelle,

If you are reading this you have finally found out that I am your mom. The hardest thing in life was making the choice to have you. A decision I never regretted. My only regret would be not seeing you grow up and being there for you. I imagine you as a little spitfire like I was when I was little -- opinionated and determined. I hope you are reading this when you are young and know all about me. Marie, your mom now, must be so proud of you. Try and cut her some slack through your teenage years. She never was as open to adventure as I was. If you are even older now, I hope you grew up knowing how much you are loved. Izzy, my love, I loved you with all my heart. You were my greatest achievement in life, and my greatest gift I could ever receive.

Love, Mom

My mom had wanted the best for me and obviously even though her relationship with her sister had become strained, she still hoped for Marie to give me the love I needed. I had never been so thankful that she wasn't here to see how I had been treated. I opened the one marked *just when you need me*. This one again was a simple one page.

Izzy,

This must be a tough day for you if you are reading this. More than anything, when days like these come along, I want you to feel my arms around you. Imagine me holding you and telling you how much I love you. You are my daughter and you have my strength. There was so much no one knew, but I can assure you I was strong right to the end and you will be also. Your life is just beginning. Allow yourself the bad days and most of all, be always ready to forgive yourself for any mistakes. Don't live with regrets, Izzy.

Love, Mom

Tears welled in my eyes. This was a note I wish I had had all through my teenage years, and college. Don't live with regrets. She was speaking right to me and I felt it in my heart. It was time to see where my life was going to take me.

thirty-eight

The house was quiet when I awoke. The sun was shining and I laid in bed listening to the birds chirping outside my window. It was a new day. Time to either close another chapter or restart it. I scrolled through my phone through social media. I once again went to Jack's profile. Nothing really new, but how I enjoyed looking at his picture. The only picture I had of him was from Christmas Eve that we spent together all those years ago. It was now or never.

I packed up my stuff and made my way downstairs. Breakfast with Gram and Papa would give a little bit more time with them. I wasn't letting them out of my life again. They had given me my mom. I was a bundle of nerves as I sat and ate. I decided to forego the coffee, trying to calm my nerves.

"Izzy, where are you headed today? Your flight isn't until this evening." Gram interrupted my thoughts.

"We've had this conversation, Gram. Just going to see if I can catch up with an old friend." I cleared my plate to the sink.

"Hmmm, old friend…I'm sure."

I turned and leaned against the sink. "What is it you're trying to say without saying?"

"Nothing. Nothing at all. Just wondering what all the secrecy is about. Haven't you had enough with secrets?"

"Really, Gram?" I laughed at her. Neither her or Papa were smiling. I sat back down. "Gram, I need to see him. I need to apologize to him."

"Yup, I thought so. You are still thinking about Jack."

I nodded. Papa reached out and laid his hand over mine. "You go get him then. Do what you need to, but you protect yourself."

"I read the letter from mom last night. She ended it with 'don't live with regrets'. Jack is my biggest regret in life. I need to offer an explanation. If he doesn't want to hear it, then that's the end of it." I squeezed Papa's hand. "I'm good, really."

I held them both close as we said our goodbyes. I was no longer running from things and I knew that we would be closer than ever. I looked forward to more stories of my mom coming from them as we talked and knew I had a lifetime to learn about her. It was bittersweet driving out of their driveway. I was excited to move forward with my newfound life, and yet it was always hard to leave the two people in my life that had offered me the most love and support through the years.

I turned my car towards the address I had put into the GPS. The closer I got, the more my stomach knotted. I stopped at a coffee shop about five minutes from the house. Using the bathroom and ordering a glass of water,

I settled down for a few minutes to relax. I had no idea what I would say to him when I saw him. Would he still be married? Would his wife, if he had one, answer the door? Was I even insane to think about doing this?

It was time. I left a couple of dollars on the table and walked to my car. I put some jazz music on as I drove the last few minutes. There were no cars in the yard, but as I drove up the driveway, I saw a car parked in the open garage. I took a deep breath and exhaled slowly. Walking slowly up the walkway, I took in the landscaping and beautiful flowerbeds. Definitely a woman's touch, unless Jack had a hidden talent that I didn't realize, which was more than probable given the short time we were actually together.

A dog barked as I walked up the few stairs to the front door. This was it…the moment of truth.

It didn't matter.

The realization hit me hard.

Whether Jack accepted, or even listened, to an apology, or whether he was still furious with me, none of it mattered. I had faced the past and survived. Not only survived, but I had conquered the paralyzing events in the past that kept me quarried in one place. My heart was healed. And whether it be Jack or Nick, or someone else, I knew I would finally be able to open my heart again.

I raised my hand and knocked. I turned and looked towards the road waiting for it to be answered.

Life was good.

acknowledgements

Fighting not being able to write brought me full circle to reevaluating life. You can't outrun your past as it has a way of catching up with you when you least expect it. Realizing the only way to break through this lack of writing was to write the hard reality of life and what we all face at some point -- regret and guilt of our choices in life.

Special thanks to Kim Law, Cindy Brannam, Jeanne Hardt and Jennifer Gatlin who pushed me to write, listened to my frustrations and are the greatest group of friends a writer could have. With every book I write, my heart swells with the support from my children, who push me to be the best person and writer I know I am capable of being. Alexa, Rachel and Nathan, you three are my life.

about the author

Emma Leigh Reed recently moved to Tennessee after living in New Hampshire all her life. She has fond memories of the Maine coastline and incorporates the ocean into all her books. She has three grown children and is enjoying her empty nest. Her life has been touched and changed by her son's autism - she views life through a very different lens than before he was born. Growing up as an avid reader, it was only natural for Emma Leigh to turn to creating the stories for others to enjoy. Emma Leigh continues to learn through her children's strength and abilities that pushes her to go outside her comfort zone on a regular basis. She is the author of romantic suspense, women's fiction and has co-authored children's books.